WRITE ABOUT YOU

JAMI ROGERS

To all the aspiring romance writers ... go for it!

Cover design © Hang Le byhangle.com

Elements Cover Design by Erika Plum

Editor: Julie Sturgeon, CEO Editor, ceoeditor.com

Proofreading: Owl Eyes Proof and Edits, www.owleyesproofsedits.com

Visit my website: www.authorjamirogers.com

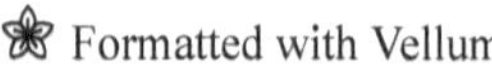 Formatted with Vellum

WRITE ABOUT YOU

JAMI ROGERS

CHAPTER ONE
ZANE

I love people watching.

I love observing the different ways people dress, walk, talk, interact, you name it. Everyone in this world acts and reacts differently and studying them never disappoints me. In fact, people watching is one of the top three ways I like to kick back and relax between novels.

I write romance.

I'm pretty damn good at it.

Too good if you ask me. It's like sipping water. Easy. Easy. Easy.

I'm so good at it that applying it to everyday life is a no-brainer. Women love to be loved. No, scratch that, women love to be noticed and appreciated. As a man, it's not hard to do either of those things. Fuck, guys, come on—say please, say thank you, open her door, buy her some flowers or books or whatever she loves, put the damn cereal bowl in the dishwasher once you're finished with it. I could go on, but you get my point. Pay attention and the rest of it, the falling in love part, comes easy.

And when you're me, Zane Rosey, award-winning and bestselling author of more than fifty steamy romance novels, you also know when and how to back off before things get too serious. Some people, like me, aren't meant for commitment. Just the fun stuff. And there's nothing wrong with that. Happily ever after isn't cut out for everyone in real life. Hence, romance novels. You get the heat without all the work or the heartbreak.

"Another round?" the blonde bartender asks me, her smile lingering and her hazel eyes focused on my lips.

I'd wink, but she wouldn't notice. She's cute. Petite. And she's also wearing a giant diamond on her left hand. Her flirting is more than likely solely for the tip.

From one "I use my job to make the most of it" fellow to another, touché.

I nod. "One more."

I open my laptop, ready to get in a few hundred more words. A thousand if I'm lucky. There is nothing wrong with my current work in progress, but I need something more challenging. I *want* something more challenging.

Maybe that's why I've been coming to this bar to write.

I'm not an idiot. When I take my computer to the bar with me, yes, I plan on getting some writing done, but mostly I just plot new scenes. I know that about ninety percent of the women who approach me to ask what I'm writing—being the only guy at our town's most popular bar, The Black Alcove, with a computer makes me stand out—and learn that I write about sex will just end up distracting me. I welcome it. Can I get my words in and still win a date for the evening? Challenge accepted.

"I knew I'd see you here tonight," Beck, a good friend of mine, pulls out the stool next to me.

I'm not the least bit surprised that he would know where to find me. Attention to detail is something all writers pick up on and seeing as how Beck is one of five of my best friends slash writing and critique partners, it makes sense. Plus, we've known each other long enough to pick up each other's habits. Mine is busying myself with work when I'm avoiding something. I know it, they know it, and here I am.

"Why change a good thing?" I say as the bartender slips me my gin and tonic.

"Sippin' Pretty, tall, please. Thank you." Beck says before he faces me.

I close my computer. It's not polite to work when your friends want to hang out. Beck has no laptop with him; he's clearly here for something other than work.

"How are you doing?" Beck asks, raising one brow as if to say, "Don't lie to me."

"Dandy." I sip my drink.

I let out a little hiss as it burns down my throat. This one is stronger than the last one.

"Are you sure about that?"

"Yes." I nod to drive the point home.

"Okay, well, in that case, tonight was fun. If that's the kind of party Hero and Nora put together just to celebrate their engagement, think of what the wedding will be like."

He's goading me. I'm not taking the bait.

I'm happy for Hero, another fellow romance writer. I really

am. He's already asked me to stand by him on the big day, and I will do it with fucking pride. I'll do anything he asks of me to help his big day go smoothly, but that's all. Just because I don't believe in love for myself doesn't mean I don't support those who do.

I know, I know, then why do I write romance?

I'll give you the short answer. Falling in love is something I dreamed of while growing up. I wanted it more than anything. So I wrote a book about a woman whom I thought was perfect for me. She was based on my first high school crush (yes, I've been writing that long). My second book was based on a dancer I met over the summer before senior year, and then my third was about the girl I met while touring the college campus here in Wind Valley. From there, it was just a spiral of girls I'd met and imagined what a future would be like with them.

Then I met *her*. The one I wanted to spend my life with. There would never be another person that perfect for me. And yet she felt that way about another man.

Now, happily ever after in my books are as close as I ever want to get to the real thing.

Beck nods, taking a big gulp of his beer.

"Look, I know you don't want to talk about—"

"Ha ha ha, oh my gosh, you're so funny, Jake. I don't remember you being this funny growing up."

I'm immediately drawn from Beck's words to the giggle of a woman behind me.

"You should be this funny at work."

I turn slowly, looking over my shoulder for the voice. It's high. Nervous as hell and cringeworthy. I swear if I turn around and she's touching his forearm, I will die of embarrassment for her.

Fuck.

And I'm dead.

I spot the hand on this guy's forearm and follow a slender pale arm to find a woman with long, straight brown hair and a pair of doe-y steel-blue eyes focused on the man in front of her. He isn't shrugging her off, but he's angled toward another guy at the table. And yet, this woman, with a button nose and high cheekbones, can't stop smiling at him. She fidgets, and my gaze drops beneath the table where she uncrosses and recrosses her legs. She's wearing a short, deep blue dress that makes her eyes pop, and although the fabric is sitting just high enough on her thighs to be enticing, it's not so high that she's intentionally trying to draw attention.

"Do you know her?" Beck asks.

"Nope."

I kind of want to, but her innocent vibe screams "looking for commitment." and even though I'm upfront with all the women I sleep with, I get the feeling this one wouldn't take kindly to just one night of fun. She's the kind who would try to change me. They mean well, but I'm not into breaking hearts.

"Do you want another round?" the waitress asks the table that has stolen my attention.

A collective yes is the answer she gets before the woman in blue and another woman slide off their seats. I turn to face the bar again when they walk toward me. I peek over my shoulder only once to check her out.

Fuck me. Those legs are long, lean, and look smooth as velvet.

I clear my throat when she stops next to me, her arm bumping mine.

"Oh, sorry," she says, looking right at me with a kind smile. Our eyes lock for only a split moment before I find my words.

"It's fine."

Beck chuckles next to me.

"I'm going to go use the bathroom. Here's my card for the shots."

The other woman, whom I can't even be bothered to watch walk away, retreats, leaving me with Blue Dress.

Technically, she left Blue Dress at the bar and not with me per se, but same thing.

Don't hit on her.

She's too kind for you.

Kind girls don't do one-night stands.

Ignoring myself, I turn to find her leaning on her elbows, watching the man at the table.

What is it about him? Jake, I think she called him.

He's wearing khaki pants and a red polo shirt. He looks like he works at Target. Not that working at Target is bad or anything, but fuck, it doesn't scream "daydream about me" while you wait for shots.

"So, have you answered your brother yet?" Beck tries to bring me back to the conversation he wants to have, but I ignore him.

I'd rather listen to the woman rave on and on about how amazing she thinks this Jake guy is than talk to Beck about my brother. That's my excuse for what I do next.

"I could help you," I say to Blue Dress.

My voice startles her. "Huh?"

I nod to her table. "With that guy. Jake, right?"

Her gaze flicks back to him.

"Oh, I don't—"

"You do. You want to get him naked."

"Jesus," Blue Dress breathes and then spins to lean her forearms onto the bar top, focusing on the mat where drinks are placed instead of looking at me.

"Look, I know this stuff, okay? I can see it in the way you look at him. You want to date him and lick his abs. It's natural."

This earns me a glare.

"I don't even know you," she says and snaps her fingers. "Oh, no that's not right. I do know you. You're Zane Rosey, the romance writer who frequents this bar over and over and uses his love language skills to take the ladies home with him only to return a few nights later looking for someone new."

Shit. Maybe I need a new bar.

I chuckle and nod. "Fair enough, but that's a bit excessive, yeah? I only come here a few times a month."

"It's enough to make a name for yourself."

"Is that from the bar or from the books?"

"Well, whatever charm you're trying to pull right now isn't going to work on me."

I won't lie. I'm digging this sass. Maybe she isn't as innocent as I thought.

"I'm not hitting on you. I'm trying to help you."

"I don't need your help."

I sip my drink and look back at her table of friends.

"Sort of looked like you do. As you said, I have love language skills. With my help, you could have that man obsessed with you in just a few weeks. Two if you do exactly as I say."

"No thanks. I'm doing just fine on my own."

She hands the bartender the credit card and then is quickly holding six shots in her hands as if waiting tables is something she does on the regular.

A glass starts to slip.

Okay, so maybe waiting tables is a part of her past. Either way, she makes it back to her group just as the other woman returns from the bathroom. They all take their shots and the man she's crushing on goes back to ignoring her.

She looks up at me.

I wink, and she rolls her eyes.

"Are you done now?" Beck asks.

I sigh. I guess my concentration for the night is already over. Oddly enough, the interaction with Blue Dress has put me off for the night. I pack up my computer and toss a couple twenties on the bar top.

"I don't want to talk about my brother."

"His wedding is next month, Zane. You really should call him."

"And say what exactly?" I snap.

Beck glares at me. "That you're going."

"The fuck I am. And stand by his side as he marries the woman who left me for him? The woman he was sleeping with before she and I even broke up. No thanks."

"It's been almost two years."

And that isn't nearly long enough.

CHAPTER TWO
WILLA

I have zero game when it comes to the opposite sex.

A part of me thought I had at least a teeny tiny bit, but after last night, it's official: I have no idea how to get a man to notice me. I've had boyfriends before. I've dated plenty, but I've never really felt that zing or whatever with any of them, so none of them ever lasted long term. I'm okay with that, but Jake, my coworker—wow, he checks off every box on my list, and when I look at him, I have no idea how to form a sentence.

Jake also happens to be good friends with both of my older brothers. So, growing up, I'd seen him plenty at their football and basketball games, but we never really spoke one-on-one. He was always just this guy I had a crush on, who I thought was perfect for me and who I thought I'd never see again once he graduated from high school and went to college.

Then a year ago, he started working at the same place as me. Fate was absolutely on my side the day he showed up.

In every way that matters, we are perfect for each other. Of course, I'm the only one who can see that as of this moment, but that's just because Jake is very focused on his work.

We work for Best You Nutrition and Chiropractic.

I work on the nutrition side, and he works on the chiropractic side. It's a fairly large clinic with twenty employees, so we don't see each other every single day, but often enough for me to know that, given the chance, we'd be perfect for each other.

I type in my notes from my last client, then hit up the breakroom for a glass of cold water, read the announcement for the new office that's opening in San Francisco and the sign for the annual company summer retreat right next to it, and then I head to the front reception desk. I don't care so much about the retreat as I do the new office in San Fran. They still haven't hired anyone to run the new office, and I want it. Badly. I have so many new ideas for this company, and although starting my own company would be better, this would be a great learning experience. Moving from Wyoming to California would be a big adjustment, but I'd do it. The dream would be that they would select me and Jake to transfer, since we are from different departments and both amazing at our jobs.

There's nothing wrong with a little wishful thinking.

Speaking of which, Jake is standing behind the receptionist's desk with a clip chart in his hands, holding up the first page as he reads it over. God, he's so pretty. From his clean-shaven face to his perfectly cut jet-black hair and the way his biceps hug his shirt. Don't even get me started on his—

"Oh hey, Willa. How's your morning going?"

As I fall out of my Jake trance, I hit my hip on the counter. "Good."

Shit, that hurts.

"You okay?" he asks, pointing to the hand now rubbing my side.

"Oh yeah, I do that at least once a week."

He flashes his perfect smile at me as he passes me to go into the back. "Well, have a good day."

"You too!" I shout with a giggle as he disappears. "Hope it's amazing."

Jesus, Willa. Seriously? Try to look a little more obvious why don't you?

"Eeek, that was painful to watch," a woman in the waiting room says.

What is it with people commenting on my life when they don't even know me? First that writer guy, Zane, from the bar last night and now this one.

As soon as the woman stands, my eyes widen, and a smile hits my lips. "Calla!"

"Willa Boston in the flesh," she grins. "How the heck are you?"

I dash around the counter and pull her into a hug.

"I haven't seen you since graduation. What's it been, five years?"

"We really left college that long ago?" she asks, her face crinkling to think about it. "I guess so, yeah."

"What are you doing here?"

"Two things, actually. One, I'm moving back at the end of the summer, and two, my brother recommended me to you."

"Your brother?" Then it occurs to me. "Oh my gosh, is Simon Scott your brother?"

She nods. "That's the one. He said you're the best nutritionist on the planet."

"Oh, that was sweet."

"Yeah, but even though I want to know all things nutrition, I like your social media accounts a lot better."

"Thank you?"

I want to laugh. Calla has always been upbeat and quick to move through a conversation. I met her during orientation at the local campus. Wind Valley College isn't very big, but boy, was I glad to have her when we lost the tour group. We were attached at the hip all four years till she went home to Melody to help her parents run their bookstore. Melody is only a couple of hours away. I should have tried to see her more.

"You should really do more with the fitness side of things," Calla says, and I'm pretty sure she's still referring to my social media account. "Nutrition is great and all, but man, the burn of a good workout, that feeling of exhaustion—well, it just can't be beat."

"I can't say I disagree." I move for the calendar. "I'm pretty booked for the next week and then we have a company retreat, but I can get with you on the Monday we are back. How does 3:00 p.m. on the fifteenth sound?"

"That works."

"Perfect. Why don't you write your email here, and I can send you a questionnaire to complete beforehand."

"Great."

The bell to the clinic rings to announce a new client. I glance up, and my heart immediately drops to my stomach.

What is he doing here?

Zane Rosey spots me instantly and grins.

"Blue Dress, this is where you work?"

"Blue dress?" I ask.

"I never caught your name last night."

"You two were together last night?" Simon, who had walked in with Zane, asks. Simon is the only reason I even know who Zane is. Simon also writes romance; it's something we have talked about during his appointments.

"Not formally. Just a quick run in at the bar," Zane answers.

I refuse to speak, so I just smile at Calla. "You'll see the email by the end of the day. I can't wait to see you again."

"Same, girl, same," Calla says, then turns to Simon and Zane. "Let's go. I'm hungry."

Zane taps the desk and waves. "See you—"

"Willa, where is Foreman's file?" Jake asks, walking out from the break room at the absolute worst moment.

Shit.

Zane's face lights up like a Christmas tree.

"Zane, let's gooooo," Calla says behind him as she holds the door open.

Slowly, he backs up toward the door. "My offer still stands." Then he looks at Jake, who is watching him, before flashing a grin my way. "I'll see you for dinner tonight, okay, babe? Have a good day."

He doesn't wait for a response before he's out the door.

Oh my god. *Oh. My. God.*

Jake is still staring at said door.

"I didn't know you were seeing someone," he says, his voice a little deeper and firmer than usual.

I search his face for my answer because I'm still a bit in shock, and I swear I see his jaw tick.

Holy shit. Is he… is he jealous?

Oh my god! This is a totally new side of him. Oh my god!

I still haven't answered when Jake's gaze flicks to my lips.

"Are you dating someone, Willa?" he asks me again.

I've never seen him look at me this way. Ever.

What if Zane is right and he can help me? Is that why he said what he said? If I tell Jake that we aren't dating, will he look at me differently?

Only one way to find out.

"Yep. Yes. That is my… boyfriend."

"Huh." He rubs his chin and stares at me.

"What?" I ask as Jake crosses his arms, now looking at the door and back at me.

"Nothing." He turns toward the back room, and this time it's him who bumps into the counter.

It's a good thing he's gone, because I have no doubt my eyes look like giant saucers. Did that just happen? Did Zane Rosey just help me make Jake jealous?

Do I want him to be jealous?

I think I do.

Shit.

Now what do I do?

"Willa, grab Jake and meet me and the others in the conference room." I startle at the sound of my boss, Arnold's, voice and then do exactly as he says.

Jake is leaning over the break room sink with his chin dropped to his chest when I come in.

"We are wanted in the conference room."

"Fine. I'll meet you there."

"Okay." I retreat to the conference room, and when Jake comes in, he sits right next to me. He's never done that either.

Do not smile like a fool. Do. Not. Do. It.

"All right, now that you are all here, I have an announcement to make. This year's annual retreat now has funds for significant others to join you. With the new office opening in San Francisco, we want to take a more family-style approach, so a show of hands for those who would like to bring someone so I can make final arrangements for meals."

Everyone's hand goes up except me and Jake.

"Okay, are you two sure?" Arnold asks as he counts the hands in the air.

I'm about to answer yes when Jake says, "Why don't you want to bring your boyfriend?"

On the spot I answer, "Because it's for spouses, right? And he's just a boyfriend. And we are pretty ne—"

"Nonsense," Arnold says. "Bring him."

Greer, a fellow nutritionist who is sitting across the table, looks at me, no doubt curious as to what Jake's talking about. After all, we, too, have been working together for more than a year and I've never mentioned a boyfriend. In fact, I never even mentioned him to her last night over drinks while Zane was right next to us when we bought shots. This should be fun.

I shrug. "Okay, I'll bring him."

"What's his name again?" Greer knows I'm lying. She's not asking in a mean girl way—we are friends—but I can tell she's entertained right now.

"Um, Zane Rosey."

Her eyes bug out of their sockets like a cartoon.

You and me both, sister. How the hell am I going to pull this off?

CHAPTER THREE
ZANE

The ignore button was a fabulous invention.

Every single time Zeke Rosey pops up on my screen, I tap that red button with joy.

You'd think he would get the hint by now.

Clearly not, since ignoring his call has only led him to call me once again. And again. And again.

This time, instead of hitting ignore, I stuff the phone between the couch cushions next to where I'm sitting.

I readjust my computer on my lap and attempt to focus on the manuscript in front of me. I thought moving from the kitchen table to the living room would help me concentrate, but it's not working. I could go sit at the desk in my office, but first I'd have to clean it off. I wouldn't say it's a mess per se, it's more like an organized mess. Even though you can't see the top of the desk, I know exactly what is on it and under which stack and in what corner.

Maybe I should go clean that room. It would keep my mind busy.

I'm half tempted to do it, but I don't. If I gave up writing every single time a scene stumped me or my personal life distracted me, I'd never finish a book again.

I take a deep breath and let it out and read from the start of my current chapter. I get about two lines in before it occurs to me that the heroine in my story is fighting with her best friend for sleeping with her boyfriend. Yeah, it was her ex, but still. I hate how eerily similar the backstory is to my real life.

I'm also annoyed that I started this book about a week after the invite appeared in my mailbox.

Is my subconscious telling me I'm not over what happened even though I am?

Because I am.

Over it.

I just don't want to go to the wedding or talk to my brother. I don't feel like rehashing the entire thing. They both betrayed me. End of story.

I open my notes document and type out that I need to make sure the resolution is very clear in the end, and then I click out of the current manuscript and pull up a different one.

Yes, the light-hearted enemies-to-lovers romcom my readers love is just what I need. It's got steam, it's got laughter, and it's got moments to make you swoon. Add in the fact that they got married on a whim one night in Vegas and, well, the words just flow right out of me.

I'm halfway through a sex scene when a notification pops up in the lower right-hand corner of my screen. *@Willa-Boston520 has started following you.* Followed by *@Willa-Boston520 has sent you a message.*

Huh.

Willa Boston. No shit. The woman from the bar and health

clinic is actually messaging me. I honestly thought I would never hear from her again.

I waste no time seeing what she wants.

Can we meet up?

I let out a laugh and type a reply.

I'm impressed you slid into my DMs this quickly.

Her response is instant.

I'm being serious.

So am I.

Zane.

Willa.

Please.

I lean back, resting my hands behind my head as I look at the screen. My guess is that the little stunt I pulled at her work yesterday worked for her and now she sees how right I was and wants my help.

I'm that good.

Lunch? I offer.

Something shorter. Just coffee. I actually don't even need that much time.

I chuckle at her response.

Tomorrow?

Perfect.

Love's a Brewing at 7 a.m.?

Great and um, if anyone asks you in the meantime, could you ... tell them you're dating a woman named Willa Boston?

The grin on my lips is unstoppable.

Desperate?

Desperately. Yes.

Her no bullshit attitude is fun. Plus, I did extend the invite first. What harm could this do?

Alright. See you in the morning.

I write another two thousand words before my seat cushion starts to vibrate.

Groaning, I pull my phone out to look at it.

It's my mom.

"Hey, Mom," I answer without a second thought. I know exactly why she's calling. I'd be an idiot not to, and as much as I don't want to discuss it, she's my mom. I'd never ignore her.

"Zane," she says in a mothering tone. It's the same one she used on me when I was avoiding a list of chores and she'd have to remind me that no matter how long I waited, I still had to do them. "I was worried your phone might be broken."

"Nope, not broken."

I save my current WIP and then walk my laptop to the kitchen table, where I leave it to grab a bottle of water from the fridge.

"Your brother tried calling you."

"I'm aware."

She lets out a long sigh. "Don't you think it's time you two talk?"

"Probably, yeah, but not today."

"Before the wedding, I hope?"

"Maybe."

"Because you're coming, right?"

"I promise I'll make a trip to see you next month, but it won't be for the wedding."

My entire family lives in Rockland, Colorado. That's where I'm from. It's a nice city, but once I came to Wind

Valley for college, I knew I'd be staying here. It's the perfect place to get that small-town vibe without it actually being a super small town. It's like a medium town, and I love it here.

"You're the best man, Zane."

I laugh and almost choke on the sip of water in my mouth.

"I didn't even call him back when he called me to ask or texted me, Mom. I'm not his best man."

"Response or not, he's counting on you."

Like I counted on him to not steal the girl I was in love with? Looks like pure disappointment for this outcome too.

"Sorry, Mom."

"Well," she says, and I can't miss the optimism in her voice. "There is still time before the big day. That leaves plenty of time to change your mind."

Doubtful.

The conversation moves quickly into talk of her garden and the tomato plant that has grown out of control and how the jalapeños just aren't growing like they used to, then we discuss my books and upcoming releases.

I'd take any subject over the one that is my brother.

Now, I just need to find a way to avoid it until the big day is over.

CHAPTER FOUR

WILLA

I think I'm going to be sick.

Is it hot in here?

I grab my shirt and tug it from my neck.

Great, I'm sweating.

I can't believe I'm doing this.

I don't really have an option.

This is so far out of my comfort zone, it's not even funny.

Oh god, and he's here. Zane Rosey is here. I don't know how to act.

He winks at me from the order line before making small talk with the older woman in front of him. She could probably be his grandmother, which is probably why she takes to him so easily and then laughs at whatever he is saying.

Jesus, is he this smooth with everyone he meets?

"You look beautiful this morning," Zane says, dropping into the seat across from me once he has his drink in hand.

"You don't have to do that."

"Do what?" he asks, leaning back and resting his arm on

the back of the chair next to him. He's only wearing a white shirt and blue jeans, but he definitely wears it better than any other man.

"Hit on me," I answer, pulling my gaze off him.

"I wasn't hitting on you. I was giving you a compliment. You look nice today."

I choose not to acknowledge his comment. I should be happy and say thank you, but I can't. If I don't say what I came here to say, the chances of me chickening out are high and I really, *really* can't afford it, and then I'll have to tell everyone the truth, and then Jake will think I'm crazy and … I'm rambling. *Rip the Band-Aid, Willa.*

"You write romance, yes?"

He chuckles, which in turn earns him a glare from me.

He drops the smile. "Yes."

"So you've written the whole fake dating thing, right? That's why you acted like the two of us were an item the other day at my work?"

He nods.

"And it works every time?"

His head volleys back and forth. "Well, yeah, I write it that way."

"But in the real world, would it work?"

The coffee cup in his hand touches his lips as he sips. His eyes never leave mine. "I have the feeling you already know the answer to that, and that's why I'm here."

I groan and drop my head into my hands. "Ithinkineedyoutoplayfakeboyfriendforme."

"Um, what's that? You were mumbling."

I drop my hands from my face and look him right in the eye. "I think I need you to play my fake boyfriend."

One shoulder lifts nonchalantly, as if my request is not unusual for him.

"Sure, what do you want me to do? Take you dinner? Show up at your place of work a few times this week? Send you flowers?"

"All of that, and then I need you to go on a four-day, three-night retreat with me and the company I work for."

His hand barely covers his mouth to stop the spew of coffee.

"You want me to do what?"

I sit up with more confidence, because he's a lot easier to talk to than I imagined the entire drive here.

"Well, you see, this is pretty much your fault."

"Ha. Explain it."

"You're timing to make Jake jealous was right before a meeting where we discussed a retreat my company is having, and this year spouses are included, and when they took roll call of who was bringing their spouse—"

"You raised your hand."

"Nope. I, in fact, did not, but Jake decided to ask me in front of everyone why I wasn't bringing you."

The laugh that escapes Zane shocks me.

"It's not funny."

"It's because he was totally calling your bluff."

"My bluff?"

"Yeah, and you clearly held your own."

I watch the man across from me for a moment as he checks his phone and drinks his coffee. He's just sitting there as if we are a couple of friends talking about work gossip instead of sitting here like me, freaking out that I quite possibly just made a complete fool of myself in front of my crush. I need help. I need a lot of help. How does Zane not see the SOS signals I'm sending?

I knock on the table to get his attention.

"Yeah?" He looks up.

"I. Need. Your. Help."

"To make this Jake guy jealous or so you don't look like a liar in front of your coworkers?"

"Both."

His brows raise with a nod as he drinks his coffee.

"Well?"

"Well, a drop-in at work or flowers would have been fine, but this retreat thing, I think you're going to have to find your own way out of—"

He's cut off by his phone ringing. I glance fast and see the name Zeke across the screen before he flips it over.

"You know what, yeah. I think I will help you. When is this retreat?"

His sudden change of heart intrigues me, and it makes me more than curious about who Zeke is, but I need the help, so I'm not about to ask and rock the boat.

"Next weekend. We leave on Thursday and come home Sunday."

"Perfect. Send me the details. What's your phone number?"

"My phone number?"

He waves his phone in front of his face.

"I guess we can keep messaging via Instagram, but texting works much faster."

"Oh, right, yes."

I take his phone and enter my digits.

He stands.

"Wait, um ..." I hesitate to find the words, so he sits back down.

"What is it, Willa?"

"I ... want this to work."

His expression goes blank.

"With Jake I mean. I like him, and as much as I don't want to admit it, you making him jealous finally got him to notice me. So, please help me make this work. I'll ... I'll do whatever you tell me to do."

He nods.

"Trust me, Willa. By the end of this retreat, he will be begging you to break up with me so he can have his chance."

I pinch my lips together to keep from grinning like a fool.

Lucky for me, my phone beeps with a text to distract me.

Wyatt: Who is this boyfriend Jake told me about? As your brother, I should have known before him, yeah? Bring him to dinner tomorrow. I want answers.

"Ohhh crap. Oh crap. Oh crap."

"What?"

Zane inches closer to look at my phone.

"Um, minor detail." I scrunch my nose as I think of how to say this. "So, this guy I told you about ..."

"Jake with the terrible style, yes, go on."

I roll my eyes. Just because his style doesn't scream sexy bad boy like Zane's does doesn't mean he has bad style, but again, I'm not going to share my opinion now that he's helping me out.

"Well, he's friends with my brothers, and it seems he's already asking about you."

A low whisper touches his lips. "All from one mini-interaction. Damn, I'm good."

"Zane!"

"Okay, so what's the problem? Just tell them yeah or whatever they want. Just keep me up-to-date on the details."

"No details yet, but they want you to come to dinner tomorrow."

"Dinner? Where?"

I cringe. "At my mom's house."

"Let me get this straight. You just asked a complete stranger to pose as your fake boyfriend, go on a weekend getaway with you, and now you're asking him to come to a family dinner."

"You don't have to say it like that." I cross my arms. "I told you this is your fault."

He shakes his head. "How do you know I'm not a murderer or something?"

"Seriously? Most people in this town know who you are because of your books. If you killed anyone, I'd know."

"Fine. Still, you should be more careful."

I ignore his comment.

"So you'll come?"

He groans but nods. "If I hadn't seen you firsthand with this guy at the bar the other night, I'd say you're trying to trick me into dating you."

"Trust me, I'm not."

"Good, because I don't date. I don't do commitments. It's messy. This whole situation we just created is the perfect example."

"Well," I stand and grab my caramel chai latte, "we don't have to worry about that. You don't date, and I don't want to date you. I want to date Jake. I don't see any trouble or mess with this so-called plan. One week, maybe a week and a half, and the two of us can part ways."

"Deal," he says and offers me his hand.

I shake it with a firm jerk.

It's only a matter of weeks before I'm finally dating my dream guy.

EEK!

CHAPTER FIVE
ZANE

"Should we go a full six or stop at five?" Beck asks as we round another corner through downtown Wind Valley.

Running is how Beck handles his writer's block, so here we are. I'd been planning on going to the gym when he called. This is one of the reasons I love my friends. No matter what, we are always here for each other. I'd rather be lifting, but he needed this more.

"What kind of scene has you stumped?" I ask between breaths. His answer will definitely determine the length of today's run.

"The black moment."

"Shit. Better make it six."

"Fuck. You're right."

We both pick up the pace.

"Talk to me about something. Anything to get my mind off it. The longer we go without talking, the more my mind stays stuck," he says. "I hate being stuck. It makes me feel like I forgot how to write."

I know exactly what he means. I also know the perfect subject to get his mind off his current manuscript.

"I've got a fake girlfriend."

Beck stops running.

"What?"

"I. Have. A. Fake. Girlfriend," I say slower.

"I heard you the first time. My *what* was referring to the fact that I need more details."

"Fine, but let's keep running and next time just say you want more details. Maybe that's your issue with the book. You know what you want to say, but you're not saying it right."

"Damn, so just rewrite the ending?"

"Give it a try. Won't hurt, will it?"

"Good point. Now spill."

We fall into stride together, and I tell him as much as I know.

"So what? You two go away for the weekend and this guy is just supposed to be jealous?"

"Basically. I'll be the doting boyfriend and make her look irresistible. Which, honestly, she's a fucking ten plus as it is. This guy has to be blind."

"Or maybe he just doesn't want to date a coworker."

That's a fair point I never considered.

"Could be. Either way, it sounds like I got a stir out of him with just a two-minute interaction the other day. Think of how much I'll help after a whole weekend."

"You don't even know this girl. Are you sure it's a retreat and not her luring you into the woods to kill you?"

"All right, you are the second person to relate me to murder. What is going on? Do I give off a kill or be killed vibe?"

"I'm just saying be cautious."

"She's Simon's nutritionist."

"Oh, wait, the girl from the bar?"

I nod. "That's the one."

Again, he stops running.

"You're not into her, are you?"

I laugh. "She made it quite clear she wants a relationship. Monogamy. Commitment. All things I don't do." And do not plan to do so in the near future either. "Plus, I told her I don't date. She knows the deal."

Beck laughs as he unlocks his truck and pulls two waters from the cooler in the back. "Says every woman at the start of the books we write."

Jesus, him too? "I think I can handle this."

"Says *every man* at the start of the books we write."

"I'm serious." I sip my water. "She's too sweet for me. I don't want to break her heart. It will be over before we know it."

Beck eyes me for a moment and then nods. "Did you make rules?"

I shrug. "It's pretty cut-and-dried."

"So if you kiss her, then what? If you have to share a hotel room, then what? What if someone wants to make plans with the two of you, then what? What's the breakup like? Are you the bad guy? Will this affect your career? Will—"

"All right, all right." I hold up my hands. "I get it. Willa and I need to make some rules. I'll mention it to her tonight, geez."

"Tonight? You're hanging out tonight? I thought the retreat was next weekend."

"It is, but her family, thanks to her brothers being besties with this guy she likes, sort of got wind of our relationship." I use my fingers as quotes for the last word. "So we are going to her mom's for dinner tonight."

He chokes on his water.

I pat his back.

"Okay, okay, so you're up against the possibility that he doesn't want to date a coworker, and she's his best friend's sister. Those are two strikes working against you."

I never really considered that either. Huh.

"I hate to break it to you, Zane, but this cut-and-dried plan you two have might be a lot harder than you think. When you see Willa, you two need to make a better plan. Stat."

"Yeah," I rub my chin. "I think we do too."

I hop into his truck as he drives me back to my place.

Even with the obstacles in place, this whole thing won't be that bad. Come on, aside from it possibly taking longer than a week or two, what could possibly go wrong?

CHAPTER SIX
ZANE

A lot. A lot of things could go wrong. Starting with this dinner with her family. I knew I should have called her before we met up here.

Fuck.

I thought I'd be a lot smoother than I'm being right now.

"So you're the one who writes porn?"

Willa's oldest brother has been mean mugging me since the moment I walked in and hasn't said a word to me, so I'm not really surprised that this is his first question. I'm pretty sure both Willa's sisters-in-law and mother and other brother have been dying to get to this question. Hell, they've asked me just about everything else they can think of. Including my shoe size.

"Wyatt! Stop." Willa rushes to my defense. "He writes romance novels."

"Same thing, isn't it?"

"Not really," Willa and I answer at the same time. We

share a look, then smile at each other. This must not sit well with her brother, because Wyatt goes on.

"It must take a special kind of man to write romance novels. I mean, isn't it just a bunch of made-up shit that no couple would ever try in the bedroom or is it realistic?"

All right, Zane, pull out all the confidence you have. I may be sweating bullets on the inside, but they don't need to know that on the outside.

"Ah, well, technically, all of it can be done in a bedroom or really anywhere. I wouldn't write it if it weren't realistic. The reviews I get sound like I'm on the right path."

"Ha, right. I'm sure they are mediocre at best."

Willa lets out a laugh and then stops immediately, covering her mouth with her hand.

"What's so funny?" her brother asks her.

"Nothing."

Her eyes meet mine, and the blush tells it all. She's read one of my books, or at least part of one.

I stare at Willa, hoping she can read my mind from across the table.

We need to create a backstory before anyone asks about it.

"So, how did this happen? When did you make it official? You've been secretly dating this whole time, haven't you? And oh my gosh, Willa, is this why you keep saying you're happy just the way things are? Because you go home to this man every night. What's your favorite thing about Willa?"

My gaze bounces from Willa's to her mom's, to both her brothers and then back at the sisters-in-laws, who are all just rambling off questions at the same time.

I feel like her brothers would want to step in and tell them I don't need to answer any of that, but no one is saying anything. Everyone is watching me. Except Willa. She's on her phone. Sweet. *Throw me to the wolves, why don't you?* Maybe she thinks that because I'm a writer, I can come up with anything at any random moment.

My phone pings, and I jump from the patio table.

"Work. I bet it's work. I'll be right back."

I stand quickly and make a beeline for the kitchen. Behind me, I hear Willa tell them that she's going to check on me.

"Damn," I say as soon as the sliding glass door is closed behind us. We both look over our shoulders at her family. They're all looking at us.

"Damn," I say again.

"At least put your phone to your ear," she scolds me.

Shit. I do it and feel dumb as hell.

"Why do I feel like I'm under investigation? I really thought this would be easier."

Willa shakes her head but smiles. "It does, doesn't it?"

"We hadn't even discussed what our story is."

"I know." She blows out a breath. "Let's keep it simple. You've been pining for me since the day you met me at the clinic. That's easy to remember."

I guffaw. "You've been pining for me since *I* became *your* client."

"No."

"Yes. It's way more believable."

"Hardly." She laughs. "You're the hopeless romantic who writes love stories for a living."

"Is that what they think of me?" I practically yell, putting my phone back in my pocket.

Better yet, is that what she thinks of me?

I shake the thought. Why does it matter? I won't see these people again after a couple of weeks.

Willa grins. "No."

Then she scratches the back of her arm and looks away.

"You're lying." I grin. I bet she has no idea she has a tell.

Her hands go to her hips, and she jabs a finger in my chest. "I'm not lying."

Another scratch and more avoided eye contact.

"Look at me and say it, then."

She laughs and shakes her head. "New subject." She jabs me in the chest again.

"Ouch!" I snap and grab her hand before she can do it again. I didn't intend for the movement to pull her closer to me, and I definitely didn't intend to pull her so close that our noses touch. I especially didn't intend to not push her away and instead close my eyes, breathing in the lavender scent that consumes her.

"Oh, don't mind me," Wyatt says, causing us to spring apart. "I just came to let you know that a bunch of us are heading to the Black Alcove for drinks. You two should join us."

"Oh." Willa waves a hand in front of her face like she's swatting away a persistent fly. "We have plans."

A twisted side of me likes watching her like this. The spontaneity of who knows what is going to come out of her mouth is entertaining as hell. "We do?"

She nods and then glares at me. "Yeah, you know, at your place." Her brows raise, and it's no guess that her jaw is clenched.

"We can do," I lean in to whisper, "that later."

"Ew, gross. Just come, okay?" her brother says, already heading back to the patio.

Once he's gone, Willa groans.

"This is way more than you bargained for, isn't it?"

"Yes, but we're in it now. May as well go all out and take you out on the town."

She palms her forehead. "Maybe this is why Jake doesn't want to date me. I'm a mess."

"You're not a mess," I say without missing a beat. "He just hasn't seen the real you yet."

She looks up, her eyes smiling just as much as her lips. "Yeah?"

"Yep, and with a stud like me on your arm, he's about to see it."

She shoves me.

"You just had to sneak in a compliment for yourself, didn't you?"

I shoot her a wink and nod toward her family.

"Come on, let's say goodbye and start the next adventure of the night."

I reach my hand out and she takes it.

"Let's do this."

CHAPTER SEVEN
WILLA

I've never been good at lying. Ever. Once, when I was six, I tried to lie to my mom that my brothers broke the front window with a football, but she knew right away that I wasn't telling the truth. In fact, I think she cut me off mid-story. I knew from that day forward that I couldn't lie to her about anything. I really did think she was the only one who would recognize my tells, but clearly, I was wrong.

I can't even begin to describe how impressed I am that Zane spotted them right away.

Still, if I'm that easy to read, who else is going to figure this out before it works?

"I can't believe this is happening."

Zane nods. "You've mentioned that about every five seconds since we left your parents' house."

"Well, this is just crazy. Who fake dates in real life? Isn't this like for the movies and books? Where do I expect to go from here? Huh? Where do I go, Zane?"

"I don't know. Anyone in your life that you hate right now? Enemies to lovers are always good."

I shake my head and glare at him. "I'm being serious."

He chuckles and then nudges my arm with his elbow as he pulls into The Black Alcove's parking lot. "Take a breath. I'm happy to help you, Willa. Besides, it's like research for me."

I shake my head. "Just don't name your next character Willa ... or Jake."

"Deal. Ready?"

He starts to get out, but I practically leap over the center console to stop him. My hand is on his thigh as I say, "Don't move yet."

He turns to face me, his body resettling into this seat. That's when I notice how close our faces are. Our lips, to be more exact. This is twice in less than an hour that we have been in this position, and my heart is racing just as fast this time as it was the last. In fact, it's beating harder at the thought of this than the reason I stopped him in the first place.

"Um, I just, Jake was walking by."

"Was he now?"

With just those three little words, the smell of cinnamon and spice surrounds me. From the gum he'd been chewing, no doubt, but it's in my mind now. That's his smell.

I like it.

"He's, um, gone now." I retreat and reach for the door handle, but Zane puts his hand on my leg this time.

"Close proximity is a given in the situation we've created Willa. Can you handle it?"

I nod.

"Good, because I may act on it. You're too beautiful not to. I just need you to remember one thing."

"What's that?"

"It's not real. Everything we do from this moment on is an act, and the two of us are going to play our part better than perfect. Got it?"

I take a deep breath, but again, nod. "I got it."

We make our way into the bar, with Zane holding my hand the entire way. I've been here dozens of times, but this time feels different. It's as if I notice the paint-splashed cement floor for the first time and the jukebox in the corner that I'm pretty sure is just for show at this point, and the stage where tonight's band is about to begin. I notice the two blondes behind the bar, laughing with their coworkers. One of the male workers grabs a blonde by the hand and twirls her, ending with a kiss. Her laughter brings an entirely new vibe to the space. Is this what it's always been like? Fun, flirty, and inviting.

"Willa, over here!" my younger brother, Austin, shouts.

Zane tugs my hand to follow him, and I stumble a little at the sight of Jake sitting with my brother. Yeah, I saw him walking across the parking lot, but I just didn't put it all together till now. We are all hanging out. On display. All of us. Together.

Zane catches me before I make a fool of myself.

"You good?"

"Yes."

"Change your mind?" he asks, and as if the universe is trying to remind of why I'm doing this, Jake glances in our direction. He looks … I don't even know. Curious? Like maybe he doesn't believe what he is seeing.

I want the look he gave me at work the other day. The one filled with desire. The one that says he finally sees me.

"I'm not changing my mind," I say.

Zane turns to continue, but I jerk him back and flash a wide grin. His lips tug to match my smile. "Why are you—?"

I press up on my toes and touch my lips to his. It's a soft kiss I'd meant to spark a little bit of jealousy in Jake's eyes, but the tenderness lasts only a split second before something else kicks in.

The moment Zane's hands snake around my waist and pull me against him, I swear my body reacts on its own. I wrap my arms around his neck, I sweep my tongue past his lips and into his mouth to tangle with his, and I moan. Yep. I freaking moan.

I'm pretty sure that sound is what makes Zane snap. His hands find my hips, and he backs me back out of the front door without looking back or breaking the kiss. Once we're outside, my back hits the wall of the building. Zane's leg settles between my thighs while one hand cups my face, tilting my chin so that he can deepen the kiss.

I've never been kissed like this. With such desire and recklessness. Every single spot that he touches me wakes up and I'm left reaching, almost tugging him close to pull him back to me when he steps away.

"Fucking hell, Willa."

"What?" I ask as I try to catch my breath. I know it's a stupid thing to ask, because what I really want to say is "fucking hell, Zane, we need to make him jealous, not think he doesn't stand a chance."

"You did not tell me you could kiss like that," Zane almost growls.

"I didn't realize it was something I needed to disclose."

"Well," He braces one hand on either side of my head, "maybe you should have."

The door swings open, and Jake pokes his head out.

I'm still pinned to the wall under Zane's gaze, chest heaving to catch my breath.

"You guys coming in?"

Zane presses off the wall.

"If I had it my way, we wouldn't, but alas, Willa wants to see her friends," Zane answers as if he didn't just give me the best kiss of my life.

And yet, the look on Jake's face says the mission I'd set out to do has been accomplished.

Yay.

I think.

"Cool, we saved you a seat." He ducks back in as Zane and I share a look.

I'm not too sure what to make of what his gaze is trying to convey, but I do know this; if anyone had any doubts about whether or not our relationship was real, they're definitely gone now.

And me—well, if Zane hadn't given me a pep talk about how not real this is in the car before that kiss, I'd be confused.

But I'm not.

So what if the guy who is pretending to be my fake boyfriend just stole my breath with one freaking kiss? I'm here because I want someone else.

That part hasn't changed.

I need to rein this in.

I push Zane back and smile. "Did you see how jealous he was?" Then I pat his chest. "Good job."

I head for the door once more.

I can be attracted to one person and want to be with another at the same time. It's not illegal. In fact, it happens all the time.

Just not to me.

Damn it.

CHAPTER EIGHT
ZANE

I haven't seen Willa since last weekend when we went out with her brothers. We've texted here and there, but only for details about the retreat. And that's fine. That's exactly how it should be. We definitely, *definitely* do not need to talk about the kiss I can't stop thinking about.

The one where I felt my entire world shift only for her to be ecstatic that it worked. The kiss did its job and made Jake want her more.

A solid example of why I do not date. Feelings are hard to control, and once they get involved, you're practically screwed.

Not that I have feelings. This is just, as I said, an example.

"What exactly does one do on a retreat like this? Do you call it a health and wellness retreat? Team building? Or something else?" I ask, attempting small talk as we drive to the hotel she provided. It's a few hours outside of Wind Valley, near Lovers Lake Lodge, which is where my brother is getting married next month.

"Honestly," Willa begins, "we just call it the Be You Annual Retreat."

She keeps playing on her phone as we talk.

"Original. What will we be doing?"

"If it's anything like last year, it's pretty luxurious. Spas, dinners, group activities. It's not bad."

"Spa. Like massages and stuff?"

"Exactly like that."

"Huh, this whole thing is really turning out to have lots of perks for me." I shoot Willa a wink, but I think the hidden meaning of our kiss being a perk goes right over her head. I don't know why I did it, maybe to see if she'd have a reaction or something to say. I'm a glutton for punishment. Of course she doesn't have a reaction. She just wants Jake.

"Yeah, totally. The food is great too. Last year, there was this steakhouse that catered one of the dinners, and I swear, I almost cried."

"Over a steak?"

"Yep."

"I'm looking forward to it."

We spent the remainder of the drive talking about everything and nothing. She tells me about a possible job opportunity in California, and even though she doesn't say the words, I take it as a hint that she needs to impress her boss. Or more so, maybe I should.

Either way, soon enough, we are pulling up to the entrance and I'm handing my keys over to the valet.

Time to put our game faces on and based on the last two times we've been on show, we need to talk a little first about what to expect.

"Okay, first things first. If they mention that we are

sharing a room, do not freak out," I tell her. "Be calm and smile."

"Oh crap. You're probably right. Is that okay with you? Sharing a room."

I smile and nod. "It's just fine with me. Is that okay with you? If it's not, then we need a plan fast. Are we old-fashioned and waiting for marriage? Is it—?"

"It's fine with me." She laughs off the answer as we step into the hotel lobby. "We are both adults."

"Ah! They are here." A red-headed man claps loudly. "Okay, let's go."

I eye the group in front of us and the fact that they are all standing in the lobby holding on to their luggage.

"Were they waiting for us to check in?" I lean in to ask Willa.

"It looks that way," she whispers back. "By the way, the crimson-haired man is my boss, Arnold."

"I have a surprise for you all," Arnold says and claps his hands once more. "To enhance our team-building skills and for my brother and I to observe the way you all work with a loved one, we are not actually staying at this hotel. Or any hotel, for that matter."

Willa and I share a look of confusion and she shrugs.

"There are three vans waiting for us outside. Let's go."

Everyone in the group starts talking at once. Even though I'm eager to hear everyone's reaction, it doesn't escape my notice that Jake is the only one here not attending as part of a couple. He's solo. I can work with that. Maybe get him and Willa a moment alone toward the end of the retreat. Probably team them up at some point. Oh, I could fake an injury before a team-building exercise and boom, they are matched up.

We load into the van with Willa and I smashed together in the back. Jake pokes his head in and, you guessed it, squeezes himself right in on the other side of Willa.

"This should be fun," he says with a big smile.

"Maybe," Willa says, looking out the window past me and barely acknowledging the fact that Jake was talking to her.

I bite back my smile and enjoy the ride.

* * *

A tent. We are legit retreating in a fucking tent.

Now, I'm fine with camping, and this is basically glorified camping because the beds in these tents are traditional beds, and they even have nightstands with battery-powered lamps, lush blankets, and a clothing rack and mini shelf for our clothes. The tents are big enough to stand up in and are in a circle to keep the group together. There is a building for us to take showers and use for bathroom breaks, but that's where it ends. Even cell service is nonexistent. A bonus for me. I'd said yes to this whole ordeal to distract myself from my brother's constant phone calls—zero service means avoiding his calls altogether. Everything else is in full camping mode. Even the cook that was hired is cooking over a firepit.

Although, cook isn't exactly what I'd call him as I stare down at my dinner.

"What is this?"

I poke at it with the wooden fork they gave me, and it jiggles back into place. I look at Willa. This is not the cry-over-me steak she promised on the drive.

"Tofu?" She, too, pokes at the food on her plate.

Across from us, Jake takes a huge bite and smiles.

I fight to roll my eyes.

What does Willa see in this guy? Now, I can tell that he's watching us because he is jealous, but I won't lie—this guy is a total dick. I'm all for helping her, but it rubs me the wrong way that he sees her now only because she's taken. What a tool bag.

I wouldn't be surprised if he hits on Willa or tries to make a move on her even knowing that she and I are dating.

Eh, okay, maybe he won't, considering he's friends with her brothers.

And I don't actually know him well enough to make these judgments.

I glance up just as he winks at Willa.

I take that back. His friendship status isn't going to stop him, and I'll judge him all I want.

"If I eat this," Willa leans in to whisper, "I mean, if we eat this, I think we should be ready for anything."

I drop my fork. "What does that mean?"

I look around the table at all her coworkers. Every single one of them has dug in like it's their first meal in weeks, while Willa and I sit here and contemplate the risks.

"It means, what if one of us can't digest well?"

"And throw up?" I ask for clarification.

"Among other things."

To this, I burst out laughing.

I draw attention to us immediately, and Willa takes a bite as if on cue.

"So good," she says with her mouthful.

Her boss looks at me and, fucking hell, I'm going to have to choke this down.

Trust me, had I known I'd be sleeping in a tent and no real

food for three days, I'd have thought twice about helping Willa hook up with this guy.

I take a bite. I'm on chomp two when I hear a gag next to me.

I keep my mouth closed as I turn to Willa, who is open mouth breathing with her hand on her throat.

"The aftertaste is … overwhelming."

Her eyes meet mine as I swallow.

The food stays safely in my stomach. "You owe me."

We finish dinner, but I'm pretty sure the entire table thinks I have zero manners as I chewed with my mouth open almost the entire time to let the taste out.

"Sleep well, everyone," Arnold announces as we are all retreating to our tents. "Tomorrow is a busy day."

Again, I shoot Willa a look. A busy day and I ate only half my dinner? I'm not expecting breakfast to be much better. This is going to be a long weekend.

I'm undressing, eyeing Willa as she peeks out of the tent, being a total weirdo. Then she rushes over to where I put my pants on the shelf thing.

"Put your clothes back on." She grabs my jeans and tosses them at me.

I toss them back. "I'm not sleeping in my jeans."

"Put them on." She tosses them back and then crawls over the bed to me. Her face is inches from mine. My gaze has already dropped to her cherry red lips. "I saw a Burger King on the way here. I bet it's only fifteen minutes walking, so eh, all in all, we could be back in an hour."

I grin stretches over my lips. "You want to sneak out … for fast food … as a health nutritionist."

"Jesus, I still need to eat, and yes, fast food. Everything

can be eaten in moderation, you know. Do you want to starve here?"

"Fair point."

So I follow my rule-breaking fake girlfriend out of the tent.

CHAPTER NINE
WILLA

"That was honestly the best burger I've ever had," I say as we make our way back to the retreat.

"It's because we were so hungry," Zane says, sidestepping a pothole in the road and bumping into me. "So, okay, fill me in on this whole retreat thing again. I need even more clarification now that the first night is almost over. You're doing it to impress the guy or the boss?"

I shake my head. "I'm doing it to get a new position with the company. The guy is here too. The retreat just happened to time itself perfectly with the help you're giving me."

"Ah. For some reason, I thought they were more connected than that."

"Yeah, I guess in my desperate attempt to get you to agree to this scam, I left out a few details."

"Seems that way. So would this new position still let you and Jake be together?"

I take a deep breath. "I hope so. We work in two different departments of the clinic. So, ultimately, we could both be chosen to head our departments at the new clinic. It would be pretty cool if that's how it works out."

"And that's what you want? To head the clinic?"

I volley my head back and forth. It never really stood out to me until just now that him being here could benefit me for the position.

"In a roundabout way. I think it's the right step to take to reach my end goal."

"Which is?"

"To run my own company. I already have a pretty large online following of women I help with fitness and living a healthy lifestyle. I'd love to own my own business where I can help them one-on-one. I don't necessarily want it online, but it's hard to get out there without social media these days. It's a good place to start, I guess."

"And how does this clinic in California help?"

"It will teach me more about running a business and balancing life with a business and—wow, I'm totally boring you."

"No, no, this is all fascinating to me. Trust me, I know what it's like to want to make something of yourself."

Yes, great, let's talk about him. We never talk about him.

"Yeah, I imagine you do. Did you always want to be a writer?"

"A writer or a romance writer?"

"Either." I sip my ice water. We had already been walking back when I realized I still had a Burger King cup. With no trash can on the way and not wanting to chance anyone finding my cup in the trash at the retreat, it looks like I'll be packing this one home with me.

I'm not sure what makes me do it, but I offer the cup of

water to Zane. He takes it as if it's a mundane action between us, sips off the same straw as me, and gives it back.

I stare at the straw where his lips just were. I've kissed those lips, and I liked it. I liked it a lot, and now we are about to sleep in a bed together and … *Wow, okay, mind, you should not be going there.*

"Honestly," Zane says, bringing me back to the conversation. "I thought I would write something more Stephen King style, but romance is just … mesmerizing. It came easy to me."

"I know I joked about it at my mother's house, but are you a closet hopeless romantic?"

"No," he chuckles. "I am not."

"Oh. Well, have you ever been in love?"

"I—shit, get down," Zane says, immediately squatting and pulling me down by the arms with him. I wobble as I steady myself in a squat and then follow his gaze.

My boss is walking around the tents with a flashlight.

"Oh, no, is he checking on everyone?" I ask.

"Like taking a tent check or something to make sure we are all here? Like some type of teen camp?"

"Yeah, just like that."

We watch in silence as he checks in at two different tents, knocking and making small conversation before moving to the next.

"Oh crap. Oh crap, oh crap," I whisper. "What happens when he gets to our tent?"

"Calm down, we can think of something."

"Like what? He's going to see us and this damn cup, and then he'll think I can't handle living a balanced lifestyle or whatever. This retreat is supposed to tell him about how I—"

"Hey, hey, stop! He's not going to think anything bad about you."

"I'm pretty sure he is. Oh god, he's getting close to our tent."

The best burger of my life is about to reappear.

"I have an idea, but you have to trust me," Zane says.

"Considering I have zero ideas myself; I do."

I feel like a teenager about to be caught behind the bleachers after a football game.

"Perfect. Now stop talking and lay on the ground. On your back."

I don't even question it; I just do as I'm told.

In an instant, Zane is crawling on top of me.

"Now, laugh," he commands.

"Do what?"

Instead of answering, he pinches my side. I let out a yelp and then start to laugh when he doesn't stop tickling me. Then, his lips are on my neck, and I can't breathe.

"Who's over there?"

A light shines on us, and that's when it clicks. Zane and I look like we snuck off to have a private, intimate moment.

"Ah, sorry, sir. I didn't think anyone could hear us."

My boss approaches, shining his light right into my face so I have to keep my eyes closed.

Zane adjusts his position, and as he does so, the cup of water he'd maneuvered between us breaks, cold liquid spilling out between our bodies.

We both let out a noise that could definitely be mistaken for something else as our clothing soaks up the ice and water.

"Oh, whoa." The flashlight flicks away from us. "You two should get back to your tent for that."

"Will do," I say quickly. "So sorry."

I'm dying inside.

My boss lets out a small chuckle. "Ah, to be young again," he says and passes right by our empty tent.

Zane and I both remain in position until we see him retreat into his tent and his light goes out.

"I think the coast is clear," I whisper.

But Zane doesn't move.

Instead, I feel his hand come to my cheek and his thumb brush over my bottom lip. I look up into his eyes, and it's like he'd forgotten where he was. He jumps up, grabbing my hand to pull me with him.

"We should hurry back."

He speed walks toward our tent, and I follow, my fingers sweeping over the spot on my neck where he kissed me. Never mind the fact that we both have giant wet spots on our pants that definitely make it look like one of us, um, got too excited—I'm too busy thinking of the rush he just gave me.

I know it's been a bit since I've been with a man, but wow. I wasn't startled or feeling shy about his lips on me. No, my body wanted more. Just like when we kissed at the bar. I wanted us to be anywhere else for just a moment longer to see what more he would do.

Zane strips his pants off the second we are inside our tent.

I freeze on my side of the bed.

The water from that damn cup soaked through his jeans, leaving the perfect wet outline of him through his boxers.

Fuck.

I look at Zane, who is now under the sheets, and then at my side of the bed.

When we got here, I wasn't nervous about sharing a bed with him. Nope. I was fine.

One little touch and now …

How the hell am I supposed to sleep knowing that ginormous thing is right next to me?

CHAPTER TEN
ZANE

Sleeping sucked.

It was just a neck.

A fucking neck.

But damn. I groan and shove my face into my pillow. Her skin was like fucking velvet against my lips, her lavender smell relaxing me enough to be in the moment for a second longer than I should have. If her boss hadn't been blinding us, I'm not sure I would have stopped. I wasn't sure her boss would have noticed us at all, honestly, but I figured anything was better than nothing. He couldn't find our tent empty, and that was the first thing I could think of.

Me. On top. Of her.

One more groan and I roll over, draping an arm over my eyes.

I still have two more days with her in this tent and fake dating her on this retreat. This is going to be brutal.

For one, I'm here to help her gain another man's attention, and two, she clearly wants to be in a relationship, and I can't give her that. One night of fun, sure, I'm her man. Anything more, no can do. I need to get her and Jake in a situation together as soon as possible.

"Zane?"

I jerk up to a sitting position and look at the entrance. Willa is standing there with her hair pulled up, revealing that sweet, soft neck of hers.

I'm so fucked.

"What's up?"

"They want to begin today's team exercise in about thirty minutes. Is that going to work for you?"

"Should be fine. I just need to shower."

"Great, I brought you a breakfast burrito." She tosses it to the bed instead of just walking it to me. Distance is probably good. Maybe she feels it too?

"What kind of meat?" I ask, and she laughs.

"Sausage. I asked."

"Finally."

After a beat of awkward silence, she ducks out.

I won't lie. I really wish the showers were a little more private around here. I could definitely use a cold one.

I eat the burrito in just a few bites and then gather my things, making my way to get cleaned up. Lucky me, I show up at the same time as Jake.

"Morning," I greet him.

He says nothing in return. He just glares at me and watches me like he wants to kick my ass.

Normally, I'd have something smartass to say, but I am intentionally here to get under his skin, so starting an argument of any kind is pointless.

"Did you have a good night?" he asks in a clipped tone.

"Not too bad." I rub my neck. "I have a bit of a kink, though. I should probably try to hit the hay a little earlier tonight."

Preferably before dinner, if it's anything like last night. Plus, it could give Willa and Jake time alone.

That's my new plan for tonight.

"Yeah, well, I'm sure rolling around on the hard dirt will do that to a person."

Rolling around in the dirt? Shit. Are people talking about that? I thought only her boss saw us. Surely, he wouldn't be spreading gossip about that.

If Willa thinks the retreat will help her get that new position, my choices for us last night might have ruined that.

Damn it. I need to find her.

"Calm down," Jakes says, clearly reading my thoughts. "I don't think everyone saw you. It was just hard not to check out what's going on when I heard Willa's infectious laughter."

Infectious laughter. I'd laugh at how gone he is for her, but he's right. Just thinking about it makes me smile.

Shit.

"Yeah, I suppose you're right. Guess we'll just keep it in the tent tonight."

I meant it as a joke. Sort of. Either way, it doesn't go over well.

"She's not a piece of fucking meat, man. She's a good girl."

Don't I know it?

"Don't worry, man. I know how amazing she is. Trust me."

Our conversation ends there as he shakes his head and disappears into a stall to shower. I do the same and am just finishing up when Arnold's voice can be heard loud and clear around the campsite.

"All right, if everyone could gather around, we need to begin the day. We've had breakfast, so next up is—drum roll, please—team mud madness! And then meditation hour before dinner."

What the hell is team mud madness?

"What's mud madness?" someone, I think her name is Greer, asks from the back.

"It's a bit like a tough mudder, only a lot smaller and not nearly as intense. Although there will be harder obstacles that will require you to work with your team or partner. I've already assigned the teams. So, please come up here and get your team's name and shirts!"

My stomach growls, wishing I could have another burrito before the day begins. What are the chances of the rest of today's meals being normal? Probably about as good as the chances of Willa and I sneaking out of here during the day or again tonight for food. Slim to none.

Speaking of, where is she?

I scan the area, but I hear her first. Her laughter. The laughter Jake is currently creating.

What the hell could he be saying that is so damn funny?

"Willa," I call out as I approach them. "Are you ready to see what team we're on?"

She looks up at me, slight annoyance touching her narrow eyes, but she nods. "Yes."

She waves to Jake, who watches Willa walk toward me. At this point, I'd say Willa and I have done such a successful job of making him want her that if I left right now, they'd hit it off.

And yet, I'm not going anywhere.

"Why did you do that?" she asks. "We were having a good conversation."

"And let him see how you'd openly flirt with another man while in a relationship? Nope. That's not the message you want to send him."

Completely just pulled that out of my ass, but it works.

"Damn. You really are good at this."

She loops her arm through mine, but I pull it out to wrap my own around her shoulders and pull her close. Then I kiss the top of her head. "You make it easy."

To this, she lets out a laugh. It's different from the one I'd just heard with Jake. It's softer and more relaxed.

I glance over my shoulder, but Jake isn't there anymore. Is it possible that she'd been faking her laugh with Jake just now? I mean, she wants his attention. I wouldn't put it past her to pretend whatever he said was funny. At the same time, for as long as Jake and Willa have known each other— hell, he's friends with her brothers—if he can't tell the difference between her real and fake laugh by now, he's an idiot.

* * *

I'm going to die.

"Faster!" Willa yells, and I pick up speed. My legs run faster than they've ever run before. I hit the mud puddle and slow down so quickly you'd think I hit a brick wall.

"What the hell, Zane?" Willa shouts with a laugh. "I'm starting to feel like your physique is misleading."

"It's not misleading, all right? I'm more of a weight-lifting type of guy. I don't do much cardio."

"I thought you said you run with your friends from time to time?"

Not into giant brown puddles.

"Yeah, I do. But it's not often."

I push my way through the mud to where Willa is waiting. Don't even get me started on the fact that she's ahead of me. I'm not upset about it, but it would be cool if she knew I was a leader too. Or in better shape than I'm clearly displaying at the moment. The only reason I'm not complaining is because stupid Jake is behind me.

I'd look back to see if he's gaining on me, but I don't want it to slow me down. Or stress me out. I don't care why I'm here. I have to finish before he does.

"Where is the rest of our team?" I ask.

I was beyond thrilled when her boss announced teams, and Jake wasn't on ours. I can't even tell you the names of her coworkers on our team—I just focused on the fact that Jake wasn't one of them.

I grin just thinking about his cringey face when he figured it out.

"Coming up close behind us. But the good news is, even though you're behind me, we are still the first two in the lead."

"Good."

I wipe my forehead with my arm. I love that Willa is competitive. She's a motivator, and I am fully into it, but I can't let her see how much I enjoy her spirit right now. Or just doing anything with her, really. As much as I'm enjoying my time with her, I can't forget that I'm here to help her win over stupid Jake.

But I can still enjoy myself. No harm in that.

I reach the end of the mud puddle, and since the mud is up to my waist, Willa offers a hand to help me. We are in the lead, so I find this is a good a time as any to have a little fun. I tug her into the mud with me.

"Zane!" she hollers, but like before, she laughs. She attempts to splash me, but I, in no delicate muddy way, maneuver out of the way. I lunge for her at the same time she lunges for me. We collide, my hand reaching for her sides to steady her.

The next thing I know, I'm very aware of her clothes sticking to her body and the way she's holding herself steady with her hand on my shoulders. Our noses are an inch away from touching, and when I close my eyes, all I want to do is kiss her. I could. We don't know who could see us, and the more people who catch us kissing in secret, well, the more believable it is, right? She and I are together.

I move my face just slightly, letting my lips brush over hers. I don't want to take advantage of the situation, but if she wants me to kiss her, I will give her what she wants.

And clearly what she wants is to kiss me back.

Her arms wrap around my neck tightly as she clings to my body, her tongue diving into my mouth. I grip her tighter, causing her body to rub against mine.

"Fuck, Willa, do that again."

She does and I growl, gripping her ass to wrap her legs around me.

I'm aware we are in a mud puddle. We are messy as hell and this is as far as it can go, but I'm here for it.

Kissing Willa is like the rush I get when I hit publish on a novel. I want more of it. I want it every day. I want it for the rest of my life.

Hoots behind us indicate that the next group isn't far behind. Regrettably, I break the kiss.

Once Willa pulls away and I'm able to pull my eyes off her, I climb out, offering her a hand to do the same.

Then we finish the race in first place.

The moment Willa hugs me to celebrate, that's when I know.

In just one week, I fell for her.

CHAPTER ELEVEN
WILLA

When the evening ended earlier than the last, I expected Zane to stick with the group for appearance's sake, but he surprised me. He excused himself to go back to our tent after dinner—veggie burgers—all while nodding toward the group and telling me to go have fun.

I know what he meant. Go talk to Jake.

And yet, even knowing that I'd have Jake's full attention if I did stick with the group, I followed Zane to the tent instead.

Well, I followed him after about five minutes, so finding him sitting cross-legged on the bed leaning back with his phone in his hands wasn't exactly what I expected. Although, I'm not sure what I expected, to be honest. For him to be sleeping? Pacing the tent with anxiety over how he's going to bring up that mud kiss?

No, that's just me.

He glances up when I step in.

"What are you doing?"

"Checking on you." I shrug.

He smiles. "I'm fine. You should go back out there. It's a great opportunity to get some one- on-one time with Jake without me breathing over your shoulder."

What if I like him breathing over my shoulder?

"Okay, what do you plan on doing?" I ask, moving into the space rather than out as he suggested.

He flashes his phone screen at me.

"Trying to get some writing in. I'd plug my computer in, but I can't exactly do that out here."

"I suppose not. I'm sorry you've had to rearrange your writing schedule this weekend to help me."

Without hesitation, he sets his phone down. "I'm enjoying myself, Willa. Make no mistake about it. I'm having a good time with you this weekend."

"Even though we're faking it?"

He nods slowly. "Yeah, but it's not all fake, is it? Everything we talk about is real—it's just our actions that aren't real."

Aren't they though?

"Right."

He picks up his phone, and his thumbs fly over the screen as he types. His brows are dipped, and his jaw is clenched.

"What are you writing?"

He groans, and my stomach instantly turns. I knew I shouldn't have said anything. I knew it.

I open my mouth to apologize for possibly ruining any inspiration that might have taken over, but he beats me to it.

"Can I ask you something?"

"Of course."

"I know there is a chance you've never read my books but

would you … never mind." He looks back at his screen and rubs a hand over his face.

"I did buy one actually. I only read about half of it, though. My schedule is pretty busy but ask me. Please. I want to help."

He glances at me briefly. "I don't know, Willa, it might be … a lot."

I smile at his nervousness. "Zane, since when are you shy?"

"I'm not being shy. I just think this would be a little over-whelming for someone who hasn't read even one whole book of mine."

I playfully shove him and sit on the bed next to him.

"I'm sure it's not so bad. Besides, now I'm intrigued. Do you want me to read something you wrote? Something no one else has ever read before?"

A smile tugs at his lips. "Maybe."

My eyes go wide. "Is it a sex scene?"

Honestly, the reviews I read said Zane can write a steamy scene that makes a woman ache—their words, not mine—and I've been curious about it. I know I just told him I'd bought a book and never finished it because of time, but right now, I'd make time if he needed me to.

"It might be a sex scene, but it's—"

"I want to read it," I blurt out, and as soon as the words are out of my mouth, it registers how eager I just sounded.

Oh well. Can't take it back now.

Going all in, I nod at his phone. "Let me see it."

He scrunches his nose, really giving it one last thought before he stands. "Okay, just sit here. I'm going to step outside. I can't watch you read it."

I laugh and lean back against the pillows to read. "What exactly do you want me to look for?"

"Oh, um, nothing specific. I just don't feel like it flows right. Like maybe it's too much. So if anything feels off to you as you read it, let me know."

"Got it."

He disappears, and the spot where he chooses to pace is perfect for me to watch him without him knowing. I bet he planned that.

With a deep breath, I begin to read.

It was at this moment that she realized she'd never been fully naked with a man before. Sure, she wasn't a virgin, but at least one piece of clothing remained on all those other times. Her bra, maybe it was her socks. Sometimes she was wearing a dress and the only thing she removed were her panties.

Not this time. This time, she was bare to him, and she loved it. The simple thought of him being the only one to see her like this made her want him even more. She'd never felt this wanted before. If he didn't touch her soon, she'd have to take care of this need on her own, and he could watch.

Damn. Let him watch? Is that what Zane is into … watching? I peek over to look at him, but he's moved.

Maybe if she told him this fun fact about herself, he would turn into a caveman and finally put her out of her misery.

"I've never been completely naked for anyone before,"

she admitted once he let his boxers drop to the floor. His cock sprang free, and her mouth watered. That was about to be inside her, and there wasn't anything she'd ever wanted more in the world.

His brow peaked at her omission. "Never?"

"Never," she repeated.

He growled and stalked toward her until she was pressed against the wall.

"Those men will never know what they're missing."

He reached down and grabbed one knee, yanking her leg to his hip so he could rub his erection against her.

"You're so fucking wet for me. I can't wait to sink into you and fu—"

I let out a breath and glance up. My eyes immediately go to the tent wall by the makeshift door. The cloth with no decor or any other obstacle on it. The wall that would be perfect for this scene. We might collapse the tent, but hey, any type of wall would be perfect if Zane ever—

"That bad, huh?" he asks, and I swear I jump five feet. "Shit, sorry."

"No, no, no, no, it's great, it's—"

"I saw how zoned out you were just now. You're bored. I was bored too. It's not intimate enough, right?"

Intimate enough? He's kidding, right?

"Shit, I knew it. Okay. I'm just going to make notes on this and move on to another scene. If I stick to this manuscript too long, I'll never get to my word count for the night."

I move to my side of the bed, and he takes his spot back.

His fingers start typing right away, moving on, just like he said.

Not me. Nope.

I'm thinking of all the dirty things he could do to me. Is Zane a dirty talker, like the heroes in his books? Are the heroines he writes the type of female he wants for himself? How has this never crossed my mind before?

"Hey." He taps the bed to get my attention. "Everything okay?"

I nod, feeling like I'm in a daze.

"Okay." He forces a tight smile and starts typing again.

I need a moment to take back control of myself, so I shake my head. "Where do you get your inspiration for the sex scenes?"

His entire body freezes.

"What?"

I point to his phone. "Do you just make them up as you go, is it something you actually want when you're with a woman, or have you already done," I swallow the lump in my throat, "these things with women?"

Suddenly, I'm very aware of the way he breathes and the way I breathe. So, basically, for a solid twenty seconds, that's all I see and hear.

"I, umm, all three, I guess."

"You guess?"

"Yep."

"Which one is this one?"

Again, the way we breathe surrounds me.

"Want."

Shit. Oh shit. Why did I ask him that?

He clears his throat and adjusts his position.

"I'm sorry. I didn't mean to pry."

"It's fine. It's not the first time someone has asked me that. I mean, it's the first time someone who is …"

Our gazes collide again. He doesn't finish that sentence, and I don't ask him to.

We both return our focus straight ahead.

"Willa," he asks. I don't need to look at him to know he's not looking at me.

"Yeah?"

"So … the scene is, uh—"

"It's good. Leave it."

I hear his sharp breath. "I will."

I should probably tell him that I didn't even get to finish the scene before I started daydreaming about it, but I'm not going to.

Had I read the entire scene, I wouldn't be imagining anything. I'd be living it.

With a man who doesn't do commitment.

That thought alone sends me scooching off the bed.

"I'll just leave you to it and go find … Jake."

Zane clears his throat.

"Good plan."

I look back one last time. He's focused on his phone again.

Yeah, good plan.

Or so it was … back when Jake was the one I wanted.

CHAPTER TWELVE
WILLA

I couldn't tell you what we did today. My brain was in a constant state of meditation. No, sorry, that's wrong. My brain was in a constant state of picturing Zane in positions I didn't need to be picturing him in. I replayed his writing in my head and wanted to reach out to touch him or find a reason for him to kiss me again.

Which is completely crazy.

So crazy.

I'm not supposed to want Zane Rosey. I'm supposed to want Jake.

The guy I've been crushing on for years. Years. And what, one week with Zane and poof! Those feelings just vanish.

Is that possible?

How could that happen?

"I don't know about you, but I'm looking forward to real food tomorrow," Zane leans in to whisper as we eat our final yummy dinner of tofu turkey sausage. I didn't even know that was a thing. "We should totally get a big sit-down breakfast at the first restaurant we see."

I nod, dazed. "We should."

Look, I'm all about a healthy lifestyle, but I'm not about cutting out food I enjoy. And right now, I'd kill for some stuffed French toast. No, eggs Benedict. Oh, it all sounds delicious.

I don't care that we've only been out here for a few days. I feel like my stomach is about to eat itself.

"Like a big ole steak and eggs. Hell, I'll shove a whole fluffy chocolate chip pancake in my mouth in one bite."

I let out a soft giggle and lean toward Zane. "Ten bucks says you can't fit a whole pancake in your mouth."

"You are so on."

"What's so funny?" Jake asks from across the table.

Zane and I both sit up straight. The question was asked so loudly that most of the table is looking at us now.

"It was just a little inside joke." Zane bumps me with his elbow. "Right, babe?"

"Right, babe," I mimic, and Zane's eyes light up as he grins.

And you guessed it; I grin right back.

At some point over the past weekend, I fell for Zane Rosey.

I'm not sure which is worse: crushing on a guy who never even noticed me till I had a fake boyfriend or falling for the fake boyfriend who made it clear that he doesn't date for real.

"Did you guys finish your worksheets?" Greer asks. She's sitting between Jake and her boyfriend, Patrick. Although, to be honest, I think she and Patrick aren't exactly on speaking terms. This retreat seems to have done the complete opposite for them of what it's done for me and Zane. Or, well, me anyway.

I grab the folded piece of paper out of my back pocket.

That's right. In our afternoon workshop, we were all given a notebook and pen to write down our goals. It could be today's goals, tomorrow, next month, or years from now. If it's a goal, we write it down. Then we were to write the strengths and weaknesses we think will help us reach our goals. The weaknesses are there to show us where to improve. Last, we were to write three things we like about ourselves.

To say my boss has covered both physical and mental aspects of this wellness retreat would be accurate.

"I feel like I'm missing a goal," I say as I review my list. Zane leans over to peek at it, but I hug it to my chest. "This is not for your eyes."

"It's not for anyone's eyes," Zane says, taking his last bite. "Seems odd to write all this down just to burn it in a campfire later, yeah?"

"The purpose is to make us mentally aware of our lives and the potential we have in them," Jake says without looking up. "So we can cherish every moment of life."

He glances up. His gaze locks on Zane's.

"I cherish more than you know." Zane's arm comes to a rest on the back of my seat.

"Good."

My gaze volleys between them and then lands on Greer, who is hiding a smile behind her hand.

"Well, this is fun. Should we get the fire ready?" I suggest, since our little group is the first to finish dinner.

"I'd love to help you." Jake stands abruptly.

"I can do it." Zane jumps up.

Again, they go into a stare-off.

"Greer?" I ask.

"Yep. Coming," she says and follows me. I don't look back.

"I can't get even one guy to look at me the way those two look at you. How do you do it?" she asks, bumping into me on the way to the firepit.

"Neither of them looks at me a certain way." I laugh.

"Oh, they do."

Finally, I look back. Both men are gone now, but if Greer's observation is true, one man is looking at me under false pretenses and the other is looking at me only because I'm taken. Both make me sick to my stomach.

"How are things with Patrick?" I ask to change the subject.

"Rocky. I mean, they were before this weekend, but I think this sort of solidified what we knew. Things between us just aren't going to work out. We're too different. Plus, he hates Wyoming, and I have no plans to leave."

"I'm sorry, Greer."

She waves a hand. "It's really fine. I'm not that sad, which I guess makes me sad." She shakes her head. "Hey, can I ask you something?"

"Go for it."

"That night we went out for drinks, you were standing right next to Zane at the bar but left him to go to our table. The next day, you said he was your boyfriend. Want to fill me in? I've been dying to ask you about it, but I've been busy."

I pause mid-step. Damn, I was hoping she wouldn't catch on to that.

"I, um …"

"He's helping you make Jake jealous, isn't he?"

I wrinkle my nose. "Is it that obvious?"

"To Jake or any other man, no. To me, someone you talk to frequently at work, yes."

"Has anyone else caught on?"

My heart races as I wait for her answer.

"No, definitely not. The rest of our coworkers are too self-obsessed, and it really, really makes me want to see what they wrote down for today's group activity."

I laugh. "I want to see what—" I cut myself off before I say it out loud.

I want to see what Zane wrote down.

We reach the firepit, and since the chairs are already in a circle, we sit.

"You like Zane, don't you?"

"Yeah, he's a nice guy."

"No I mean, *like* like him."

"Oh." I look over my shoulders to make sure no one is around. "He doesn't do the whole commitment thing, so it doesn't matter how I feel."

"Total bummer, Willa."

I nod.

Bummer indeed.

"Maybe he'll change his mind. I wasn't joking. That man looks at you like he could eat you for dessert. I don't think it's an act either."

A smile tugs at my lips no matter how hard I try not to let it.

"If that's how he looks at a woman in real life, I bet the guys in his books are wildly dominant."

And just like that, I'm brought right back to the scene I read yesterday.

It's probably best that tonight is our last night together.

* * *

Hours later, and shocker! —my mind is still racing with images of that scene Zane wrote. Images of him and me in the scene. Of us acting out every single word.

My body basically twinges with the need to bring it up, just act on it, or … I don't even know. I just know that my body feels like it's about to combust, and with each little movement between the two of us in this bed, I ache for him to touch me.

Zane. Not Jake. Not the guy that I came here to woo or whatever you want to call it. Let's be honest, any thoughts of Jake and I as a couple are long gone at this moment. Not saying I've forgotten him completely, but right now, today, this weekend, my body craves only one man and he's lying right next to me.

It's probably the fact that we're stuck in proximity, so my mind is confused, but I could do this, right?

I could have a fun one-night only fling. Then, when the week rolls around and I'm back at work and it's me and Jake working side by side, everything will be back to normal.

Yeah.

Yeah.

The bed moves as Zane adjusts his position, and I'm not sure which is louder, the rustle of the sheets or his groan.

I kid you not, that groan speaks to my soul.

He's feeling exactly what I'm feeling. There is no way he can't be.

He shifts to his back, so I shift to mine.

His arms fall to his sides, so I do the same.

Silence.

And yet the moment his pinky touches mine, my heart races and my body temperature rises. My nipples perk up, and the spot between my legs wakes up.

Jesus. It was just a pinky swipe.

He moves again, this time just enough that our arms are flush against each other.

Just turn to your side, Willa. You do it, he'll do it, and then he will kiss you and you can have everything your body desires right now.

Do it.

Do it!

"Willa," his rough voice croaks out.

I clear my throat and try to speak in a calm breath.

"Yeah?"

"I …"

He what? He what!

"Nothing."

"Tell me," I say before I can think twice about it.

"It's nothing, really. This weekend is just getting to me. I haven't been this one-on-one with a woman in a while, and my mind is—"

"I want you to kiss me again," I blurted out. "Wherever your mind is, mine is too."

He groans even louder. "Don't say things like that."

"Why not?"

"Because I … I'm not the guy for you, Willa. In the long run, it's not me."

"Well, it's a good thing I'm not talking about the long run. I'm talking about tonight."

"Fuck."

"That's what I'm thinking."

He chuckles, rubbing a hand over his face. "Willa, have you always spoken this openly about what you want?"

I shake my head, somehow just realizing that we are still lying on our backs, gazing up as we talk. "This past week I've felt different," I confess. "Like I'm finally going after what I want and it's about damn time I did too."

"And what do you want tonight?"

I choose this moment to roll to my side. He does it quickly after me as if I had pulled a string.

I reach for his face, my gaze staring into his deep blue eyes. He isn't saying a word, but I can see it in the way he looks at me. He wants this too. He wants me. And he wants to give me what I want.

Don't ask me how I got all that with a look, but I did.

My lips tug into a grin, and he closes his eyes.

"I want you to make me feel good, and I want to make you feel good. After tonight, we go back to our lives."

I've barely let the last word fall from my lips before he scoots closer, his free hand grabbing my hip to pull my body against his then crashing our lips together. His chest is bare, so I can instantly feel how hot his skin is. It warms me to my core, and the feeling of comfort it brings me has my hands clawing at him, making sure I touch every last inch of muscle.

"God, your lips are like fucking silk," he says, peppering

kisses down my neck. He reaches for the hem of my shirt and starts to lift it. But then he pauses.

"What is it?" I ask between breaths.

"These tents are thin," he whispers.

"So?"

I totally get what he's saying, but still.

"I can be quiet," I say and then bite his ear.

On a growl, he nibbles my collarbone and takes my shirt off.

I'll be honest; I have no clue if I can be quiet. I've never actually had to. Shoot, I've never had sex that even came close to making me feel the way I do when Zane kisses me. So, yeah, I'm curious how much of what I just said is a truth and how much is a lie.

He pops one of my nipples into his mouth, and I cry out.

I lied. Clearly.

He pulls back, our gazes colliding. "Willa, if you can't be quiet, I'm going to have to stop. Is that what you want?"

God no. Never.

I shake my head.

He leans in close to whisper in my ear. "Good."

He goes back to showing my chest all the attention, and I swear he's driving me insane to see if he can make me crack again.

I gasp once, but outside of that, I hold it together well. That is until he slides my pajama shorts down. His fingers tease me right over my panties. When I can't take it anymore and I'm ready to make noise, I jerk away from him and take control.

I flip him to his back and straddle his lap.

I reach my hand into the waistband of his shorts and grip his hard length.

Yes, this is what I want. I rub above him, but he stops me.

"Hold on, Willa. I didn't bring anything with me."

I pause and then groan, dropping my chest to his.

"I didn't either."

But we can still do other things.

I begin to grind on him once more, but again he stops me.

"Willa, I swear to you that you are amazing, and I—"

"It's fine." I know where he's going with this speech. I can't say I would argue with him. What would happen if I got a taste? Would I be able to stop after just tonight? Would he? Would this end with me and a broken heart?

"Look, Willa, I'm sorry."

I take a deep breath and then look at him. I smile. "It's really okay, Zane. We're good, okay?"

His eyes focus on mine for a moment before he nods.

"Okay."

I roll over and close my eyes.

I can't wait to go home tomorrow.

CHAPTER THIRTEEN
ZANE

I'm a jackass.

Even though Willa said we were good, she still hasn't spoken to me all morning except to ask if I was ready to load up in the vans.

I left her to flirt with Jake the other night for a reason. To get her off my mind. To get some space between us and put him on her mind. Not that I was on her mind, of course. I wouldn't know that. I didn't plan for her to come to the tent and for me to share a sex scene with her. Dammit. What the hell was I thinking? And then last night … fuck. This retreat wasn't for her and me to get closer. It was for her and Jake.

Idiot of the Year goes to Zane Rosey.

We should talk about last night. But I also know this was only temporary, and what good would come from any conversation about what almost happened? Nothing. We'd be right back here in my truck, driving to Wind Valley in silence. And in the end, the outcome would be the same: I stopped what could have been the best night of my life.

Like I said, this thing between us has to come to an end at some point. We may as well discuss that, right?

"So," I say and tap the wheel with my thumb. "Should we talk about how we want to play out our breakup?"

The silence that has filled the car since we left is immediately broken with a snort.

"Oh, right. Yeah. The breakup. What did you have in mind?"

I hesitate before I speak. "I'm not really sure. I was hoping you had an idea."

Honestly, when we started this whole thing, I figured a simple fight outside her workplace would work, or maybe she has an even simpler plan, but I think we played our part a little too well the past few days. So well that people would question how Willa could move on so quickly after we break up. Public is better, yet quiet and discreet feels more the direction we are headed right now.

"I know we said we'd end it after the retreat." She sighs. "But maybe we should keep it up for at least a week or something."

"I could do that," I say, a little too eagerly.

"Great."

She looks at me with a forced smile. I return the sentiment.

More time with Willa is okay with me.

Wait. This isn't real. This is just an act. I can't get caught up in it. Last night is a perfect example, and I can't forget why this whole thing started. For her and another guy. Shit.

It's not like keeping it up for another week means we have to physically hang out.

How many times do I need to remind myself of this?

As if I needed an even bigger reminder, my phone, which has been plugged in since we got into the truck after it died last night, starts to ring.

Zeke.

And that right there was exactly what I needed. I press ignore and give my attention back to Willa.

"So I'll just drop you off, and then we let a week go by and tell everyone it's over. That should work. I guess, um, you can call me if anything comes up."

"Oh." She looks out the window and nods. "That. Sounds. Great."

I breathe in deeply and let it out slowly.

Do not ask her what's wrong. You know what's wrong. Asking her means caring and caring means feelings and we do not have them.

Yet, we do.

A little.

Fuck.

"I'm sorry about last night," I say without another thought. "I let things go too far. We had a deal, and I crossed the line."

She lets me suffer a solid thirty seconds before she says anything.

"You weren't the only one in the bed, Zane, but you're right. I got caught up in the moment and the act of having someone in my life, and it was wrong of me to use you like that."

"You wouldn't have been using me. If we had been any other place, I wouldn't have stopped you."

"And what would have happened after?" she asks.

I shrug.

"Exactly. This is for the best."

I nod and once again tap the wheel.

"Yeah, I don't know, something about this still feels weird. Or unresolved?"

"The weekend or last night?"

"Last night," I answer. "I know we are both saying it's fine and it was the right choice to make, but damn, Willa, I think you're fun as hell and I like being around you. I know we are going to break up," I say the last two words with air quotes, "but I want to keep hanging out. As friends."

"Ugh, gross. The friend speech," she says with a laugh. "I'm sooooo lucky."

I nudge her and she swats me away. "I don't want to make a promise I can't keep, and friends is something I can promise."

She lets out a deep breath. "It's hard to be mad at you when you've been nothing but honest with me. And a little because I kind of like hanging out with you too."

"I knew it. I knew it this whole time."

The laugh that she lets out is my favorite. It's the relaxed one that hits me right in the chest.

I can be just friends with Willa Boston. In fact, I accept this challenge.

* * *

All right, here we go.

As soon as I dropped Willa off at her house, I didn't go home. I drove straight to The Black Alcove bar and plopped my frustrated and flustered ass down onto one of the barstools. I got my computer out and begged the bartender to plug it in since it died over the weekend.

I need to be here. To be in my element. My zone. My happy place. Whatever you want to call it. Not only am I itching to write more than a few measly hundred words from my phone, but I'm ready to get Willa out of my system.

Does that make me a jackass?

I was getting caught too far in the moment with her. The more time we spent together and the more time we were alone in that tiny tent, the more I wanted her. More than anyone I've ever wanted in my life. I don't care how cliché that statement is. I've never felt like that, and it's safe to say it's all due to the situation we put ourselves in.

Yes. That's exactly it.

Not even five minutes in, a redhead slides up next to me.

It's a Sunday night, and due to the bar closing early, there aren't a lot of people. Which means there are a lot of seats to choose from. Yet she chose the one right next to mine.

I'm not an idiot. I know what this means. What she's intending to get from this night.

I turn, flashing my best grin.

"Hey," I say.

As soon as she smiles back, it hits me. Nothing. Absolutely nothing. No urge to keep the conversation going or an urge to pull out my best new one-liners to see if they actually work before I put them into a book. No urge to crack a joke to see her smile.

Shit.

I pack up my bag like the building is on fire, tossing a twenty on the counter to pay for my undrunk soda.

I leave without looking back.

As soon as I'm in my truck, I know I need to go home. It's the smartest choice, but inside, my heart aches knowing that I've been apart from Willa for almost an hour now. An hour. That's it, and I freaking miss her.

I miss someone who wants another man.

Time. Yeah, that's all I need.

No matter what she says to me, we were caught up in the moment. Caught up in the moment. It was just the moment.

If I keep repeating it and rephrasing it, maybe it will stick.

I lean forward and pull out my phone, my thumb working as if it has its own set of controls, and search for Willa's contact number.

Should I make sure she's getting settled in okay?

Just say hey?

Tell her I had fun?

I grin thinking of how we snuck out to get fast food at her health and wellness retreat.

And it was her idea.

And the mud race.

Her lips.

Her smile.

That dimple that sneaks out only when she lets out a good, deep laugh that hits me right in the soul.

I click off my phone.

It was all an act for stupid Jake.

I helped her do that.

Now, I just need to let her go.

The redhead steps out of the bar, walking to her car, but she pauses as if she senses my gaze on her.

If there is one sure way to get Willa out of my system, this redhead is exactly what I need.

Yet I don't move.

Tomorrow. That's when I'll get Willa out of my system.

Tonight, well, I'm going to just enjoy the memory of her.

It's one of the best I've had in years.

CHAPTER FOURTEEN
WILLA

I'm a liar.

I'm a full-blown liar. Twice now I've lied to Zane: when I said I could be quiet, and I wasn't and then yesterday in the car ride home when I agreed to just be friends. Yes, because I want to strip down and lick all my friends naked. Not.

It's the first day back at work since the retreat and I'm in a daze.

"Willa, are you listening to me?"

"Huh?" I slowly turn to Jake, who is waving a hand in front of my face.

"Are you okay?"

"Oh, yeah, yeah, just tired, I guess."

"How can you be tired after the retreat? It was so relaxing."

I keep a smile on my face, but I'm dying to ask him what retreat he was on, because the one I was on was anything but relaxing. I don't ask him, though, because he's been finding reasons to talk to me all day.

Which is what I've wanted for months now.

So I'm happy, right?

You'd think I would be more excited about this new constant interaction between us. The more he talks, the more I keep hoping that something will click between us. That something inside of me will say yes, this is the man you want. Not Zane. Not the guy who told me from day one that he isn't interested in a relationship. God, is there something wrong with me? I mean, if a guy tells you that, you should listen, not become more attracted to him just because he's honest with you.

"Willa, seriously? Are you paying attention?" This time, Jake lets out a small laugh. "Maybe you should go home, grab something to eat, and get some rest."

That does sound nice.

I nod.

"And when you're back, we can talk more about having the catering company who catered the retreat meal plan for the clinic."

The what who now? No. No way.

I burst with laughter. "That's a good one."

Jake looks confused, so I stop laughing.

He was being serious.

"Yeah, we can talk about it, sure."

Or not. Oh my gosh. Zane is going to love this.

I glance at the clock—it's almost three o'clock. I have one more appointment today. It's with Calla Stone. Gosh, she was just in here a couple weeks ago, but it feels like ages. I'm looking forward to seeing her. I need something normal to happen in my day.

"Hey, Willa," Greer says, passing me on her way to the break room. "Any plans this weekend?"

"It's Monday."

"Well, I'm just curious. Do you have plans?" Her brows bounce, and I roll my eyes.

"Maybe."

Jake must hate our bubbly tones because he leaves the room.

"Seriously, though, what's the plan between you two?"

"It's—"

"Willa, your next appointment is here," Jake says quickly before closing the door behind him.

"Yeesh." Greer shakes her head. "He doesn't like you dating or even talking about Zane."

"I guess not."

She eyes me for a moment, and I have no doubts that she can tell my thoughts about Jake have changed. I, well, don't care anymore if he likes me or not. And I should. I should be counting down the days till Jake asks me out. Zane made it clear that he isn't available, and no matter how much I wish that weren't the case, it is.

"Talk later?" I ask because it really sort of would be nice to talk this out with someone.

"I'd love that."

I make a mental note to ask her about Patrick too.

"Hey," I greet Calla as I step into the front lobby. "Ready?"

"Oh," a devilish smile touches her lips, "you have no idea."

I laugh her response off and lead her into my office, where I like to have the first consultation.

I close the door behind us, and we both take a seat while I pull up the questionnaire she sent me.

"Have you ever been to a nut—?"

"Why are you and Zane fake dating?"

I blink. I stare. I can barely breathe.

Dammit. Is it still fake dating if all these people know it's fake?

"My brother told me. Don't worry, it's a secret I'm keeping. I'm so in love with this story and I haven't even heard it yet. Come on, please tell me everything. I mean you—"

A knock at my door interrupts the moment, and I breathe a sigh of relief.

"Come in."

"Hey, you forgot the chart for … is everything okay?" Greer asks, probably taking notice of the deer in headlights look I don't doubt that I'm displaying.

I glance between the only two women who know the truth and say the first thing that comes to mind. "I want to date Zane Rosey for real, but he doesn't do relationships, and the whole reason we even started hanging out was because I do want one. Granted, it was with someone else, but things have changed. What am I supposed to do now?"

Greer's eyes widen as she smiles and enters the room. She shuts the door, taking the seat next to Calla. They grin at each other.

"Start again, from the beginning," Calla says.

"Do not leave out a single detail," Greer adds.

And so, I tell them everything.

"You know," Calla says, "I think he likes you too."

"Oh, how could he not? It's so obvious," Greer adds.

"But if he did like me, why would he fight it?"

"Um, because he's scared of commitment." Calla rolls her eyes. "Duh."

"Yeah, he said he doesn't do it. I don't know, I always thought that although people do have that issue, when it's the right person, doesn't that change things?"

"Not for everyone. Do you know why he doesn't date?" Greer asks. I shake my head, and we both look at Calla.

Her hands go up in surrender. "I have no clue. He's my brother's best friend, and I might be able to notice things about him, but I don't *know him,* know him."

"Can you find out?" Greer asks.

"I might be able to."

"No, no," I interrupt. "I don't want to be snoopy. If I really want to know, I can ask him. We still have to stage a breakup, so I need to see him anyway."

I pick at the corner of my desk and frown.

Stage a breakup. I'd rather not, but really, what can I do? Zane made it clear that friends are all we can be. I should respect that. Especially because he has been nothing but honest with me from the start.

Ugh. Which, like I said, makes me like him even more.

Another knock at my door makes us all jump. We start to laugh just as Jake pokes his head in.

"Oh hey, sorry, I can come back."

"No, no." Greer stands. "We were just finishing up."

Calla starts to say something—clearly, we haven't even started her appointment—but instead smiles wickedly.

"Call me if you need anything, Willa honey. Breakups are hard, and I'm here for you."

"You and Zane broke up?" Jake asks, and I swear his entire demeanor perks up. He steps farther into my office.

"Let me take you to dinner tonight. We can talk about it or not."

I'm speechless. One for Calla's quick thinking and two for the fact that Jake was so quick to ask me out. I'm heartbroken or should be. What's the rule on when it's too soon to ask someone out?

Greer and Calla say their goodbyes as my absent response hangs in the silence.

I catch Calla's look as she mouths "do it" from the doorway.

"I—"

"Look, I know I should probably wait and give you time to process things with you and Zane, but to be honest, I don't want to miss my chance."

Aw hell.

I don't know what Calla's plan was, but maybe instead of dwelling over a man I can't have, I should think of the one I can. Maybe all I need to do is give Jake a real honest chance, and I'll forget all about Zane.

"I'd love to go to dinner."

"Great. I'll pick you up around seven?"

"Sounds good."

He winks and leaves the room.

Only one thought occurs to me as I sit here and think of this turn of events.

Zane winks way better.

Damn it. Tonight better be one hell of a date.

CHAPTER FIFTEEN
ZANE

I'm faking it.

My fingers tap loudly against my keyboard as I gaze over my laptop at my closest friends who look just like me right now, except they are probably actually writing.

Not me. I have a Word document open, and I am typing, but not real words. Only a lot of nonsense that I'll delete later. All I'm doing is making enough noise to make them think I'm making progress over here.

I'm not a fan of pretending. Not in real life, in writing, and especially not in bed. Why fake anything when everything in this world can change?

Yes, Zane, why fake anything?

"Time!" Beck says, and the whole group sighs. Well, everyone except Hero. He's still typing like a madman. He would too. As the only one of us who is genuinely in love, his writing streak has been off the wall lately.

Good for him. Really, good for him. I'm not bitter. I have

no reason to be. My writing is perfectly fine. So what if that's not what I was doing today? I'm not on deadline or anything. I'm ahead and my books are thriving. So it must be something else.

"I'm almost done with this scene," the current writing guru states.

"Take your time," Beck says, looking at me over his laptop. "Did you set a new record?"

The guffaw I let out is louder than I expected.

"Me?" I ask.

"Yeah, you were typing louder than I've heard anyone type, and I assumed you were on a roll."

"Oh, yeah, the words were just flowing right out of me."

"Flowing! Yes, that's the word I was looking for," Hero says and then leans back. "Done."

"Glad I could help."

"Me too. Now, tell us why you're being so sarcastic about your word count today."

"What?"

All eyes fall on me.

"We aren't stupid, Zane—we all felt you staring at us. You never look up when you're in a writing zone."

One after the other, they cross their arms and keep their focus on me.

I'm not sure if it's a perk or a flaw that, after ten years of writing together, they obviously know my habits. I can't even be mad. If it weren't for these guys and the support we have for each other, I wouldn't be as successful in my career as I am today. Now, I'm not over here winning author of the year like Hero did, but I was an author in the running and that's something to be proud of. Not to mention I've never had a book not hit *The New York Times* bestseller list or that I've been featured in *Lovers Magazine* at least ten times and as the most popular romance readers magazine, I think—ugh, they're all still staring at me.

The crap these guys would give me if they knew I wasn't writing because my mind can't stop thinking about a woman. I can hear it now. Hero would be ecstatic to have one of us on his page, Beck would be happy as hell but envious, Simon would tell me to be cautious, Graham would probably just chuckle, and Tobias would tell me the secret to keeping a woman happy is to be her best friend. To be her best friend? Ha. Does he not hear himself?

"Well, we're waiting," Hero says.

I let out a long breath as I consider what to say about Willa.

"Do you think that it's a reach to have a couple meet in a bar, never speak, but somehow know to meet the other one in the bathroom for a quick hook-up?" Graham asks. My grin is Grinch-like.

I love when someone changes the subject for me.

I meet his eye across the table, and one by one, the rest of our writers do the same.

Talk about our lives, yes, we do that, but we all know that when your mind is in problem- solving mode on a work in progress, you have to hit it while it's fresh.

"How far into the story is it?" Simon asks.

"Is this the first chapter?" Beck says at the same time.

"Bathroom sex. That's new for you," Tobias adds.

"I'm trying to switch things up."

"That's good for you, man," Hero adds, and the room falls quiet.

"Any input?" Graham asks. I look up at his question to see him staring at me.

"From me?"

"Um, yeah, you. You write the spiciest scenes out of all of us."

"Not lately," I grumble, and I swear it's like I just announced I'm never writing again. Laptops close, notebooks slap shut, and chairs screech as they turn to face me.

It would have been smarter for me to say anything else. Now the conversation is back on me, and I have a feeling I won't be able to get out of it this time.

"What happened with Willa?" Simon is the first to ask. After I told Beck about the fake dating arrangement, he'd mentioned it in the next writer meetup. It's not bad they all know, but they are romance writers. I should have known they would be invested.

My head jerks back on instinct. "Nothing. What does she have to do with me not writing a spicy scene?"

Yes, keep the topic on writing.

"Because you'd rather be living them with her instead of writing them."

"Now that," I say and point at Graham," is reaching."

"Something clearly happened," Hero points out as he crosses his arms. "Tell us so we can help you."

I may as well just tell them. If I don't, they'll hound me till I do. I'll start with the first thing on my mind.

"I let Willa read a sex scene from my latest novel, and I'm pretty sure she imagined it as us, and now I can't write a sex scene without thinking of her."

No one speaks.

It makes sense. Knowing Willa was reading my words turned me on as I paced outside our tent. I'd walked back in to her blank stare, and at first, I thought maybe she was bored, but every day that I play that moment over and over, I'm starting to think she was imagining us in the scene. Or, at least, I hope she was.

Fuck. Me.

Suddenly, all the guys start talking at once.

"What happened after she read it?"

"Why did you let her read it?"

"What did she say?"

"How do you know?"

"Did you act it out?"

"Why didn't you tell us?"

"So are you two dating for real now?"

I step into the kitchen, setting my computer down and then dropping into my seat. "Nope, nothing. I thought it sucked and wanted an outsider's opinion. I just … fuck, you guys know I don't date. Period."

Wide eyes surround me. "Stop staring at me. What do I do?"

"Ask her out, duh," Tobias says, and the others nod in agreement.

"What did I just tell you?"

"People change," Beck says. "You are people."

I shake my head and open my computer. "That's a stretch."

"How is that a stretch?" Beck asks. "It happens all the time. Look at Hero and Nora."

Everyone looks at Hero, who has just taken a giant bite of

pizza, a piece of pepperoni hanging half outside his mouth. He smiles and shrugs.

"That's a special case," I say.

"For him, maybe. This is your special case. Ask her out. If she says no, she says no. You can move past it, but at least you'll know."

I don't answer. He has a point. But am I ready to change my ways?

"Hold on," Hero says once he's done chewing. "Are you scared she'll turn you down?"

"No," I answer quickly.

"I think he is," Simon says.

"Me too," Graham adds.

"You're like … our most confident bachelor of the group and I … oh shit. Are you going domestic?" Tobias asks.

"Yes! Finally!" Beck cheers.

"Stop, all of you."

"Hold on, hold on," Hero says. "Are you all worked up about this because something already happened, and you want something more to happen?"

"I told you, nothing happened once she read it."

"I'm not talking about when she read your sex scene."

"I …" I can't even come up with the words, and once that little fact is clear to everyone in the room, they all start speaking at once again.

"Dude!"

"What?!"

"You didn't tell us!"

"What the hell happened between you two?"

"Why are you keeping secrets from us?"

"I knew it!"

"I don't know, okay? All of this is new to me, and I don't know what I'm doing, but yeah, we've kissed a few times. It was inevitable. It wasn't real. It was all for show."

Beck snort laughs. "How do you not know what's happening? You write this trope at least twice a year."

"It's not the same as living it. Besides, once again, I do not date."

How many times do I need to repeat it?

"You didn't date because you hadn't met the right woman. Willa is the right one for you."

"Guys, it's been like two weeks since she and I started hanging out."

Beck groans and slaps the table. Then he points at every computer on it. "That's legit what we do. It can happen. Trust me."

I'm not saying that they are right, and I should date Willa, but I will entertain the thought that perhaps it could be different with Willa. She's fun as hell and smart and motivated and fucking gorgeous beyond words. And yet, it still remains that she wants another man.

"It doesn't matter. We were fake dating for a reason. To make another guy jealous. It worked. She got his attention. We should cut ties and leave it at that."

"So you two haven't spoken since you've been back?" Simon asks.

"Nope. We are planning to meet later this week to fake break up."

"Here's a thought," Beck adds. "Don't. Don't fake break up. Ask her out."

"I'm not asking her out. Don't you think if it were that easy, I'd have done it by now?"

"But you've thought about it?"

I nod. They'll all know if I'm lying.

"Anyway, I've got to get going." I glance at my watch and close my computer. "I have a takeout pickup calling my name and a house that is quiet where I can think."

"About Willa?" Simon chuckles.

"And how are you going to ask her out instead of breaking up with her?"

I look at Beck and roll my eyes. "Sure."

We say our goodbyes since a couple of the other guys are heading home as well.

Asking Willa out wouldn't be the worst. She is pretty awesome, and we have a blast together and the sexual chemistry is on fucking fire. It makes sense. Not all women are like my ex, so why not?

And like they said, if I just do it, I'll know, and I can move on.

I jog into the restaurant to pick up my food but stop dead in my tracks at a table directly behind the hostess stand. The one where Willa is sitting with Jake. On a date.

What the hell? A heat creeps into my neck and my heart clenches.

We haven't even staged a breakup and she is already out with him?

Fuck.

I glance away, waiting for the hostess to appear. Any fucking time would be nice, because I swear Willa's presence is haunting me, chanting "look at her, look at her" and I really don't want to.

But I can't help it.

Of course, because this world is out to get me when it

comes to the opposite sex, Jake says something that makes Willa laugh. I swear I stop breathing. It's her real laugh.

My food appears, and I hightail it out of there.

Single.

That's who I am, and I need to remember that.

CHAPTER SIXTEEN

WILLA

One hell of a date is an understatement. One hell of a horrible date is more accurate.

"And then once I could bench press double my brother, I knew I had to go into a field of study that helped with taking care of the human body. We take our bodies for granted, and I want to help people see how beneficial health and nutrition is for them."

Turns out, the only thing Jake and I have in common is where we work.

Oh, and apparently, I compare all men to Zane.

Why did he have to set the bar so damn high?

I barely laughed for real when he was talking about my brother right before his benching story. This date is not good. Jake and I are … not good.

"I'm sorry. Are you feeling okay? Do you want to leave?" he asks.

I shake my head but don't look up from my lap. Where would I look anyway? At Jake? So I can feel sad all over again for the clear as day list of poor choices I've been making?

"I was thinking," Jake says in a tone that hints he's trying to change my obviously low mood. "We should see if we can add gym memberships to the clinic in Cali."

Oh hell.

"You know what? I think you're right. We should go. I need to go."

"Oh yeah?"

"Yeah. This might have been too soon. You're a really great guy, Jake, you are, but I'm not ready to date anyone else."

He presses a thin line of a smile and nods. "You'll let me know when that changes?"

I can't bring myself to say the word *yes*, so I nod and smile.

And that is how the date I'd been waiting years for ends and how I end up driving straight to Zane's house.

I'm not crazy, am I?

No, I'm not.

If he isn't happy to see me, I'll keep this chill. If he is happy to see me, well, I'll stick to my plan. Which really isn't a plan, I guess. I just know that I want to be around Zane. Friends, more than friends, in any form he will take me.

Zane opens the door as I'm still pacing by my driver's side, trying to decide whether this is a bad idea or if I should just calm down and talk to him.

Which is clearly the only choice I have now.

"Hi," I say with a wave and clasp my hands together in front of me.

He gives me a half smile and leans into his doorway.

"Willa," he greets me. His eyes narrow slightly, and the full smile I've grown to admire in a short amount of time appears. "What are you doing here?"

I hold up the bag in my hand and smile. "I brought ice cream."

"What, no dinner?" he says jokingly, and I freeze. My heart beats so fast and loud I swear he can hear it. Do I tell him I was with Jake? That our plan worked, but it also didn't because Jake is not the guy for me.

I open my mouth to say that, but what would I say next? That it's him. He's the guy I want. I can't do that. He doesn't do relationships, and I can't forget it.

Friends. I'm here as a friend.

"That's for another night," I say with a wink.

He laughs. "Another night? I'm not so sure we are good enough friends to hang out on a regular basis yet." His voice is laced with humor, and my reaction feeds off it as I hand him the bag and follow him inside.

"Well shoot, tell me what I need to do to be a good enough friend," I say and bump his hip with mine.

He freezes with his hand on the bag, a blank expression on his face.

I hadn't meant for that comment to be so flirty, but I'll admit, I like how confident his stunned silence makes me feel. Shocking Zane Rosey is becoming a new favorite habit of mine.

"What did you bring?" he changes the subject, unloading the mint chip and cookie dough ice cream onto the counter and grabbing two spoons. "Oh good, it's real ice cream and not frozen yogurt."

"Ah! Speaking of healthy food, Jake wants to hire that

company to prepare meals for the clinic. I swear, I thought he was joking when he suggested it. I wanted to call you as soon as he mentioned it, but I wasn't sure that was allowed with our not-quite-good-enough friendship."

"Wait, you're telling me you were with the guy you're crushing on, holding a full conversation, and you thought about calling me?"

I bite my lip and dig out a cookie dough chunk. Yes, I guess I did. Now that he mentioned it, I was more excited to tell Zane about the meal prep thing than I was about going to dinner with Jake.

I glance at Zane, who is studying me with a scowl. Instead of answering his question, I move on to, "Oh, by the way, you're off the hook about thinking of a whole breakup strategy. I took your advice and told him it happened on the drive home."

His scowl deepens but what was I going to say to the guy who made it clear he doesn't want a relationship beyond friends? *Yeah, I told Jake we broke up but turns out I want you more.*

No thanks.

"So how was your day?" I ask.

I glance around his kitchen, taking in the modern look and the white and black jars that read flour, sugar, coffee, and tea, and then at the sign above his sink that reads Save Dishes, Eat Out.

Neither of them has any significant meaning to me but being in his house with him, I'm comfortable. I don't feel nervous or anxious or like if I say the wrong thing, he'll judge me for it. I feel like I can be me.

I don't think I'll be able to make up too many more

excuses to see him now that I've finished our split without him, so I need to come up with a new plan. A new reason why we should keep hanging out without spooking him into thinking it's because I'm crushing on him now, even though this is clearly the case.

He takes a bite of his ice cream and then licks the spoon. I'm so focused on the movement of his tongue that I don't notice the ice cream on my own spoon has dripped to the counter and right onto a save the date card.

"Oh no." I grab a paper towel, rushing to clean the photo.

"Don't. It looks better with the smudge."

I look down and see that it's covering a woman's face. The guy in the photo looks eerily similar to Zane.

"Is that your brother?"

He nods.

"How fun. He's getting married."

Again, just a nod. But this one comes with raised eyebrows and an eye roll.

"I sense a story," I say. "Tell me about it."

"It's a long one."

"I have time. Besides, you're a writer, give me the hard-cover back blurb version."

He grins, clearly thinking it over.

"I haven't spoken to my brother in a couple of years."

"What? Why not?" I pull the invite toward me and see that the wedding is next weekend. "Oh, I get it. You're trying to decide whether you should go."

"Oh no, I'm not going."

"Why not? Two years is a long time. Maybe it's time to mend what's broken between you. I'm sure whatever came between you has long since been forgotten."

What if he doesn't tell me what happened? If he doesn't elaborate, that's a sure sign I should ditch the entire friends idea, too, right? What if he—?

"His fiancée was my girlfriend, and she cheated on me with him."

Ohhh shit. He told me. And, wow, that explains a lot.

"That's horrible."

It is.

"It is what it is. I'm not even mad about it now, but it's been so long and, yeah, maybe I'm a little bitter that things between them worked out this well."

"I don't blame you. Wow."

"So yep, I'm not going."

I understand what he's saying, but a part of me wishes I could do something to make him feel better. He said he's not going, but the dip in his brows as he looks at the photo says he's conflicted. Maybe if he didn't have to go alone, his answer would change.

"I think I know what you need to make it through this wedding."

"Willa, I just said I'm not going."

I ignore him.

"You need a girlfriend."

"That's actually the last thing I need."

Ouch, but it doesn't stop me.

"I meant you need a fake girlfriend. Someone to be there with you and distract you if things get rough. Lucky for you, I just happen to know a girl available for the role."

His grin tugs at my heart. God, I thought shocking him was my new favorite thing—turns out, making him smile is now in that number one spot.

"I don't know."

"Don't you want to see your mom? Or Dad?"

He nods.

"And you want to make amends without looking like you've secretly been hating them all these years for being happy."

He rolls his eyes again but nods.

"That's where I come in. I'll be the girl you're madly in love with, and you can come up with some bullshit excuse about just living in the moment and how you should have called years ago, but you wanted to give them space or something."

"Did you just make all that up?"

"Like I said, perfect for the role."

"Some of my friends are going since they are his friends too. I wouldn't be completely alone. So I don't know if that's smart."

Oh, he has a point, but still, my offer stands.

"Well, I do think it's smart. I'm the perfect getaway excuse. Think about it and let me know. You helped me, and now it's my turn to help you."

And it is. I really do want to help him.

But I'm helping us too.

There is just something different about me and him when we are together. I'm not ready to give it up yet, and if a little role reversal is what it will take to make him see that too, then here we go.

We finish our ice cream and I head home.

A gut feeling tells me I won't hear from him again, and that's that. It's probably for the best, anyway. I'm leaving in a month or so and he doesn't date. It's not like—

．　．　．

Zane: I'll pick you at 8 a.m. sharp this Friday.

Ahh!

Willa: *wink emoji* Can't wait. Babe.

I grin and lie back in bed.
　　Another weekend with Zane Rosey. Don't mind if I do.

CHAPTER SEVENTEEN
WILLA

I had no idea that Zane's brother was getting married at Lovers Lodge. It's a few hours from Wind Valley, and it's one of the top wedding destination venues in the country. Although weddings are what they are known for, they offer so much more. Hiking, water sports, tennis, horseback riding, to name a few. And even though I'm here with someone who isn't actually my boyfriend, I'm here for whatever romance vibes this place has to offer. And the lake at the back of the venue is seriously calling my name in this ninety-degree July heat.

Zane opens the passenger door of his truck and offers me a hand. I'm totally capable of getting out on my own, but I don't mind any extra moments of him touching me. I haven't seen him since the day I showed up at his house offering to be his girlfriend. A whole five days. I learned a lot in those days, and the fact that I missed being around Zane is at the top of that list.

Gosh. Am I a bad person? Zane made it clear he wants to be friends and that nothing should happen between us, and yet here I am, thinking that if we spend more time together, he might change his mind on dating.

Wow. Listen to me. All this because I want him to like me back?

"Do you want to get checked in and put on our swimsuits and lay out by the lake, or do you want to rent jet skis or something? Go hiking? Or …"

"Hiking is good," I answer quickly.

Another thing I learned while being away from Zane this past week is how attracted to him I am. Hiking involves more clothes. Right now, my self-control needs more clothes on both of us. As much fun as we could have in swimsuits, hiking is probably the wiser choice.

"Sounds good. Where did you put your hiking boots?" he asks as he hauls my bag from the bed of the truck, clearly not catching a hint of the war inside my brain.

I nod. "In my apartment."

Shitballs. I knew I forgot something.

A smile stretches over his lips. "Well, that's a pretty inconvenient place to put them before a hike three hours from home."

I catch my reflection in his aviators as he speaks. Well, well, well, look at all those pearly whites.

I shift my gaze to the front doors.

"Yes, it is."

He chuckles.

"So, jet skis or lay in the sand? Or we could fish. Or we could go horseback riding. They also have a bar and restaurant with a menu to die for. I bet they have a steak we could try over here. You do owe me one of those."

He laughs again and slings my bag over his shoulder, leading us inside.

Jet skiing equals splashing each other around and not talking. It keeps our hands to ourselves, but I'd rather talk. Laying in the sand involves talking, but we'd both be half naked. Horseback riding is … I don't trust an animal that big, and drinking is probably what I need to calm my nerves, but not a good idea.

"Laying out in the sun sounds great."

Wish me luck.

"Awesome," he says, giving the valet his keys. "Let's get checked in, change, and then order drinks to take with us."

"Perfect."

Check-in goes smoothly, and the receptionist informs us that we are the first in the wedding block to arrive. I can tell from the breath that Zane lets out that was exactly what he needed to hear. I know this weekend isn't easy for him. Good thing he has me. I'm here to help him relax.

In any way he will let me.

Oh god. Listen to me. When I was crushing on Jake, I never thought of all things I wanted him to do to me or the things I wanted to do to him, and yet here I am, not even able to walk a hallway without thinking of how I can—

"So what side of the bed do you want?" Zane asks from just inside our room.

"Um, it doesn't matter. The left side is fine," I say quickly and step around him.

He looks at me, opens his mouth like he wants to say something, but then nods. "Good choice."

Oh yeah, it's great. Of all the things I thought about this weekend, sharing a bed simply slipped my mind.

Okay, Willa, get your shit together. Where did the cool and collected woman go?

She's back in Wind Valley, daydreaming about this trip.

Zane walks in and sets my bag on the luggage rack before he ducks into the bathroom.

I hear his phone beep a couple of times before he reappears.

"A few of my friends just pulled in, and they rented a boat for the weekend. Are you up for that?"

"Yes."

"Cool." Like before, he watches me for a moment, but then returns to his phone to text them back, I'm sure.

As soon as he's finished in the bathroom, I grab my suit to go change. I have to pass Zane to get there. My intention is to shimmy past him, but the swim trunks in his hand suggest he had the same idea as me. So when he turns to return to the bathroom, he bumps into me.

If I take one step, my nipples will brush his chest.

"Everything okay?" he asks, not stepping back.

I nod.

"Are you sure? Because I don't like the awkwardness between us right now."

"You feel that, huh?" I bite my lip.

"I do. So it's probably best we just put it all out in the open, right?"

"Right?" I repeat with hesitation. Why do I get the feeling I'm not sure I know what he's talking about? I'm curious as hell, though.

He touches my chin and gently urges me to look at him.

"We're attracted to each other, and truth be told, if you were my real girlfriend, I'd have you naked on the bed, with my head between your legs in a heartbeat."

Suddenly, I'm very aware of my nipples.

Good thing all my swimsuits have padding.

Hell, okay, I can handle this. He's a dirty talker. I can do this. I'd probably get off quicker than I have in my entire life if it ever came to that, but that's okay. Maybe I can do it too.

"Umm." I let out a breath. "I don't think people have to be officially dating for that."

He closes his eyes and inhales. "Willa."

I close that last bit of distance between us and press my mouth to his.

Yes, there she is! My amazing, bold, and confident self.

His hands snake around my hips, smoothing down over my pants to cup my ass and lift me to wrap my legs around him. He turns for the bed and sets me down. Slowly, he pushes me back, his body pressing into mine as his tongue invades my mouth. I let out a little moan.

He jumps back, rubs a hand over the scruff of his chin as he studies me, and then groans.

"Oh god, I can't believe I'm going to say this, but fuck, we need to go to the beach."

"Why?"

"Because I didn't bring you here to have sex. I brought you here so we could … I want you to have a good weekend. I want us to have a good weekend, and people are waiting for us."

"Sex sounds like a good weekend."

Especially for a woman who hasn't had it in more than a

year. Shit, for a woman who hasn't been touched by a man in more than a year until Zane.

He growls. "Willa, I'm trying to be a gentleman here."

I scoot to the edge of the bed and stand. We're so close that I nudge my nose against his. I don't want to sound desperate, but the teasing is fun.

"Try a little less," I say and then step around him. "I'll get my suit on."

When I look back, he's pinching the spot between his eyes and nodding. "I hope you brought a one-piece."

"Nope."

"Fuck."

* * *

Zane's friends are a freaking hoot. Yes, I said hoot. I don't remember the last time I laughed this hard. From what I gather, there are six of them. Probably more, no doubt, but these six are close. Only four of them could make it this weekend. To my surprise, Calla came with her brother Simon and his son. Having a friend is definitely nice. Especially one who knows the arrangement Zane and I have.

"I'm so thrilled to have another girl around. Two, I guess, now that you 're here, Calla." Nora, Hero's fiancée, smiles as she sips her spritzer.

"You have Natalie," Calla says.

I learned Natalie is Nora's best friend, but Natalie is also Tobias's, one of the close six, best friends. I haven't met Tobias yet. It's a little hard to keep track of all the names and connections, but I'll get it.

"Aunt Calla!" Grey, Simon's son and Calla's nephew,

moves from the back of the boat where the guys are sitting to the front where us girls are laying out. "Can we jump off those cliffs?"

Calla just about spits out her drink. "What cliff? No. I mean no."

"They aren't that big."

"You're only ten. No. It's not happening."

"She said no!" Grey yells and heads to the back of the boat. It's not a big boat, so his yelling is pointless, but he's a kid and he's having fun, so no one is going to correct him.

Beck is the first to reply. "Oh, come on, let the boy have some fun."

"You're not part of his family. You do not get a vote," Calla snaps. "Ever."

If I had to guess, I'd say she's rolling her eyes under her giant square tortoise sunglasses. Not only have I learned a bunch of names today, but I've also noticed that Calla does not care for Beck, and Beck, knowing this, loves to pester Calla.

Every time they bicker, Zane and I share a look.

Holy sexual tension.

"Why don't Willa and I jump first and then we reconsider?" Zane says.

I raise my hand before he's even finished speaking.

"Um, like Beck, I'm not a part of Grey's family, so my opinion is moot."

"Get up, Willa," Zane says, and I hadn't even noticed that he moved next to me.

"I'm not jumping in," I repeat and attempt to contain my smile as he grins at me.

He leans forward slowly, one hand on each side of my head. "Get. In. The. Water."

Then he nibbles on my ear.

I shove him off me and stand. "There are kids present," I whisper-snap at him.

Chuckles from both ends of the boat surround me, and I smack his chest. "You did that on purpose."

"I needed to get you up. Now, go."

"If I do this," I point to everyone on the boat, my gaze landing on Simon and Grey, "he gets to jump too."

Simon raises his hands in surrender. "I never said he couldn't. I just said he could do it if Calla did it too."

"Ha, you knew I'd say no."

"You set me up?" Grey says and slugs his dad, who is now laughing. "Aunt Calla, come on!"

"Fine." She groans and the two of them jump into the water, Zane and I following right behind them. We swim to the cliffs and climb up the top. As soon as Calla and Grey jump, I look over the edge and start to head back down.

"Where are you going?" Zane asks.

"Back to the boat."

"Why?"

"This is not for me," I say, but Zane grabs my hand.

"What's stopping you?"

"Um, the height, duh."

"I didn't think you were scared of anything."

"I'm scared of a lot of things. This is one of them."

"Jump with me."

"No."

I shake my head, but I stop—the look in his eyes renders me speechless.

He offers me his hand again.

"Jump with me?"

I'm not so sure he's talking about just the cliff anymore.

"Aren't you scared?" I ask.

"Terrified, but if I have you with me, I think I can do it."

And that's all I need to hear.

I lace my hand with his and step up to the edge.

Here goes nothing.

CHAPTER EIGHTEEN
ZANE

I'm fucking gone for her.

For Willa.

I knew it before today but watching her with my friends and how she fits in with all of us confirms it. She's different, and I need to find a way to convince her that I'm her guy. Not someone else. Not stupid Jake. Me.

But even then, what do I have to offer her? I'm no good at commitment, and how does it make me look when I said I didn't date and yet now I want to? Or is this a lust thing where I need to be with her and then decide?

No, no, don't be a dick. You like her.

Earlier in the room … shit. Wanting to date and have a real relationship is different from just being attracted to someone. It's no secret that Willa and I are attracted to each other. But that doesn't matter, does it? Just because her body wants mine doesn't mean that at the end of the day, we can be a real couple.

Who am I trying to convince? I'm not cut out for real life

love. It's as easy as that. Talking to her and being upfront with how I feel is the right thing to do.

But hell, she wants full-on commitment. Am I ready for that? What would I even say? If I don't even know that much, addressing this subject with her is pointless.

All I know is that I want to be around her. I want to hold her hand. I want to be the guy she turns to for everything in life. Either it will work out or it won't.

With my track record, chances are it won't.

Shit. There's no point in bringing up if the result is a broken heart, and I'm not just talking about hers.

We head in from a day of boating, and I have every intention of going back to the hotel and ordering room service and spending the evening just the two of us, letting whatever happens happen. Mostly to be with her but a little because I want to avoid any run-in with anyone in my—

"Hey, man." My brother's deep voice carries in the lobby of the lodge as he joins us.

I freeze, and Willa places her hand in mine. She can sense that something is off.

"Zeke," I say on a steady breath. "Big weekend."

Fuck, really? That's what I went with?

"It is. I'm really glad you came."

He glances between me and Willa and clears his throat.

"I'm Zeke, Zane's brother."

"Willa, I'm—"

"This is my girlfriend," I say firmly and pull her closer to me.

Zeke nods. "It's a pleasure."

He looks back to me with a forced smile on his lips.

He is about to bring it up; I know it. He's going to do it right here in front of Willa.

"We need to—"

Willa tugs on my arm, cutting me off briefly, before saying, "I need to use the ladies' room. Please excuse me."

So much for being my buffer and for avoiding my family. Then again, standing here while the three of us exchange a lot of awkward glances doesn't sound all that thrilling.

She leans in to hug me and whispers, "Give him five minutes. I'll be right back."

And then she presses her lips to mine, her entire relaxed demeanor seeping into my body through her kiss, before walking away.

I'd talk to my brother over and over again if it meant little moments like those.

A simple kiss here, a hug there, whispered moments. I want all that with Willa.

Does that mean I'm ready?

I rub a hand over my face. What am I doing?

"I know that feeling." Zeke nods toward Willa. "You got it bad."

I narrow my gaze and cross my arms.

"Do you need something?"

He clears his throat. "Thank you for coming."

"I honestly wouldn't be here if it weren't for Willa, so you can thank her."

"I will. Ugh, look, I'm really sorry about everything that happened. And I—"

"I didn't come here for an apology," I cut him off. "I came here because …"

"Because it's been too long."

I resist the urge to roll my eyes. "Yeah."

"I'm not sure where we go from here," he says, but then offers me his hand, "but I'm game to figure it out if you are."

I stare at his hand, noticing Willa exit the bathroom just behind him. She smiles at me, and I swear, for as few words as my brother and I just exchanged, I know that from this moment on, everything will be just fine.

I shake his hand, and his shoulders relax.

"I should get back, but I'm so happy you're here, Zane. I mean it. You're my brother, and I love you."

I nod. "Go find your bride."

"Okay." He grins and starts to back up. "After the wedding, I want all the details."

"On what?"

"On how you fell in love with Willa. Duh. Trust me. Even if it happens in a way you never planned, it doesn't take long to know you've found the one."

Is he right? Am I in love with Willa?

No. In books yes, two weeks to fall in love? Totally. Real life? No way.

She steps up to me and I lean in to kiss her cheek.

She smiles.

"What was that for?"

"For being you," I say, and then I lace our fingers.

She nudges me and looks toward the reception hall.

"Come on, boyfriend, we have an appearance to make."

An appearance. That's right.

Because it's not real to her. It's an offer she's fulfilling, and as soon as this weekend is over, she'll go back to another guy.

To Jake. The guy she was on a date with earlier this week

and has still to mention to me. Because she wants him and not me.

God, why do I keep forgetting that? No matter what happens between us, physical or not, the result is the same. It ends with her with Jake and me … not with Willa.

As it should be.

"Where do we have an appearance to make?" I ask, my mind brushing off the negativity and trying to get back into the moment. She thinks we need to make so-called appearances only because I haven't told her how I really feel. If she doesn't know, I can't be upset about anything she does or says.

"I don't know. Just out and about, right? You want them to see that you have a girlfriend, so let's go shower and get ready and let them see."

She leads me toward the elevator, pressing the button like her life depends on it.

The doors open and we step in, luckily riding alone to our floor.

"I know we are fake dating," I say and then clear my throat. "But I …"

She turns to look up at me slowly. "You what?"

"I, um—"

"Oh wow, look at this." She points to the floor in the elevator. "How weird that this is the same floor in the California clinic pictures. Weird. right?"

California. Fuck, that's right.

My heart aches at the thought. Willa. Jake. California. That's her end goal.

"You were saying?" she prompts me on.

I shake my head. "It doesn't matter. I'm just caught up in the—"

I don't get in another word before she kisses me. I should stop her like I did before we went boating, but why would I? This is what I want. Clearly, she does too, right?

Instead of breaking the kiss, I deepen it with a flick of my tongue and then lift her to wrap her legs around me and press her to the wall. This is my favorite way to kiss her. With her in my arms and her legs wrapped around me. The way our bodies cling together is like a secret language. They can't survive without each other.

"Kissing you is one of my new favorite things to do," she says on a breath.

I kiss her again, but the doors to the elevator open, causing us to both jump back.

Another hotel guest, a man old enough to be my grandfather, steps in to join us.

Willa and I exchange a glance behind him and wait for our floor to arrive.

As soon as it does, I'm fully ready to pick up where we left off, but Beck pops out of his room.

"Oh good. There you are. Are you coming to the rehearsal dinner? It's in like thirty minutes."

I'd planned to skip it so I could avoid, well, running into my brother. Now that that's over with, maybe it won't be too bad.

I look at Willa.

On the other hand, taking her into the room sounds much, much better.

"Of course," she answers when the decision clearly takes me too long.

"Good. Hurry up. If I get left alone with Calla again, I swear I will ghost you all."

Willa laughs and my heart swells.

"That's my friend you're talking about."

Beck looks her right in the eye.

"Yep. Sure is. I don't care. Don't leave me alone with her."

Willa laughs again and tugs me toward our room. "Give us thirty minutes."

I can work with that.

Beck gets on the next elevator, and I reach for Willa once we are in our room.

She backs out of my touch.

"We have to get ready and thanks for conveniently forgetting to tell me the rehearsal dinner was tonight."

I groan, ignoring the wedding comment.

"You said thirty minutes."

A devilish smile hits her lips. "It'll be worth the wait. We need to get ready."

"Can we at least shower together?" I ask.

She shoves me back and disappears into the bathroom with an evil laugh.

I'll take that as a no.

Still, I can't help but smile. We may not have it all figured out and we're adult enough to know and understand it can't last, so with that being said, whatever is happening with us, I'm here for it.

CHAPTER NINETEEN
ZANE

I've never been nervous about bringing a woman to meet my family, but tonight is different. This is Willa. Willa is different.

I rest my hand at the small of her back as we ascend the stairs to the private room for the rehearsal dinner.

Willa met my brother earlier, but it was quick. Now, though, my entire family is going to bombard her with questions. I have no idea what they are going to say or what they could ask her. A mild sweat breaks out on my forehead.

Why am I nervous? I know how to hold my shit together, but again, this is Willa. I don't know what we're doing, but I'm not ready to lose her yet, and my crazy family might be the exact reason on why she's reminded that at the end of this weekend, she goes right back to stupid Jake.

I should probably stop calling him stupid Jake. For one, I'm an adult, and two, it could slip out loud enough for Willa to hear.

But the fact remains that Jake is—

"Are you okay? You're being quiet." Willa pauses at the top of the steps and moves in front of me.

I open my mouth to tell her what I'm thinking but stop. How would it look if a few weeks ago I was telling her not to get attached to me and now I tell her I'm freaking out about losing her? Yeah, not happening. Instead, I go with, "A little warning before we meet my parents—my mom is probably going to cry."

"What? Why?" Willa asks, looking around us as we step into the room as if a woman in tears is just going to appear.

The room isn't decorated by any means. It's a typical upper floor of an industrial style bar with three long tables to my left and the bathrooms at my right. The bar, where a sign reads His and Her Drinks, is directly ahead of us. Past the tables is a buffet line for the dinner with a chocolate fountain included.

A server comes up with a tray of champagne glasses.

"Good evening. This isn't a formal dinner. Dinner and dessert are to be served at your leisure throughout the night. The bar is open, and all tips have been covered. Enjoy your evening."

Slowly, Willa and I each take a glass and thank him.

"This is laid back. I like it. Now why will your mother cry when she sees me?"

"Because one," I sip my drink, "I actually showed up for this thing, and two, because not only is one of her boys getting married, the other is bringing a so-called girlfriend."

I cringe. I have no clue what to call us.

Friends?

Friends who kiss?

Friends who kiss and the guy knows she will end up with someone else?

I tip the rest of my glass back and cough at the burn.

"Don't say so-called girlfriend."

I glance over at Willa, letting her words sink in.

Do I ask what I should call us?

Hell, we've only kissed. That means nothing. Besides, she needs a man who can give her everything she wants. I'm perfect for right now. That's all.

Fuck. I can't even keep it straight. What do I want?

To be around Willa as much as she will let me. That's all I know.

"Oh, look at that!" she says and points to the chocolate fountain at the back of the room. "How embarrassed would you be if I stood there all night and skipped the real food?"

Her excitement hints that I'm possibly the only one over-thinking this thing between us.

"Embarrassed?" I laugh. "I spot an open table right in front of it that we should 100 percent claim for our own."

"Deal," she squeals and walks a little faster.

We reach the fountain and examine all the choices. Fruit, cakes, Rice Krispies, and more. Basically, anything you can think of to dip in chocolate.

Willa goes right for a Krispy square. She stabs it with one of the mini sticks provided and then smothers it. A little chocolate drips to her chin as she takes a bite.

"Whoops," she says, swiping it away. She lifts her finger to her mouth, but I grab her hand and stick it in mine instead.

Her eyes widen as she watches me.

I slowly pull my lips away and groan. "We should definitely take some of this back to the room with us."

She doesn't respond with anything but a rushed nod.

"Zane!" My mother's voice comes up behind me.

"Showtime," I whisper to Willa, and the smile that was on her lips fades for just a slight moment.

"Hi, Mom," I say, turning to give her a hug.

"Oh, I'm so happy that you're here." Her arms are like a vise around me. "It's been so long."

Her grip doesn't loosen. "Mom, this is Willa."

I manage to change out the introduction, and it's a good thing too. My mother instantly lets go of me.

"Willa." She smiles at my girl. "I love that name."

My girl. Whoa.

"Thank you."

"I'm Alice, Zane's mother." She glares at me. "I know I taught him better manners than to not introduce people."

She did, but if Willa is around, it seems I'm not as on top of my game as I normally am.

Understandably.

"Oh, trust me, Mrs. Rosey, he's very well behaved."

I choke on a laugh and then stop the passing waiter for three flutes of champagne.

"Did Zeke rent out this room?" I ask.

"He did. He wanted it to be private. Isn't this venue breathtaking? You two should keep it in for your wedding."

Alcohol spews from my mouth and Willa pats my back.

I'm legit struggling over here on what the hell is happening between us and my mother has us engaged.

Fucking hell, Mom.

"Too soon to swoon over the idea of another wedding and grandbabies?"

Now we are having kids. This is just great. This is exactly why I was nervous. My family is going to scare her away before we even have a chance to be friends. If, you know, that's all I want.

"Oh, Mrs. Rosey, you are too sweet. We don't have any wedding bells in our future. Just day by day for us. We're having fun. No rush."

Ah, and now I know where she stands.

It's good. Nothing serious. I can do that. I can be fun. I'm a fun guy.

If that's all she wants, I can do that.

"I know, I know. Oh! I'm just so happy to see you, honey. Now, I better go make some more rounds. It was a pleasure to meet you."

"You too."

With another death grip hug, my mom leaves us.

"Well, she didn't cry. She did deem us engaged with kids on the way, though."

At her teasing tone, I pull her at the waist toward me.

"Your mother wouldn't do that?"

She huffs. "My mother would have had a marriage license waiting on the kitchen table. I'm still shocked she didn't when you met her a few weeks ago."

She kisses me then, right in the room full of my friends and family.

"Now, shall we get on with this night or what? Because I don't know about you, but I'm really looking forward to the moment when we go back to our room—oh hey, Calla," she says and backs away from me.

They quickly start talking about their dresses for the big day tomorrow, but my gaze meets Willa's.

I heard you.

I rub a hand over my mouth to hide my smile as the rest of my friends join us.

Damn. I can't remember the last time I was this happy.

Just then, the couple of the hour steps into the room. A perfect reminder of exactly how long it's been since I pictured myself as anything other than alone.

For good reason.

Every time I think I've found the one, they end up with someone else.

I force a smile but grab another passing flute of champagne. I gulp down the one I already had and this one within seconds.

One night. I can have one with Willa. After that, I'll let her go and let her get back to the life she has planned.

It's as easy as that.

* * *

"I like your family," Willa says as soon as the elevator doors close. I press the button for our floor and nod.

"Yeah, they weren't too bad tonight. I'll claim them."

In fact, the entire night after that first encounter with my mom was anticlimactic. Everyone got along just fine. It was like the years of not speaking never passed. I did notice, however, that Willa never spoke with the bride, Mandy. Was it because they were both busy with other people, or was it intentional?

Doesn't matter, really.

"You and your brother seemed to get along pretty well."

"Yeah, it was a good night."

I lean back and drop my gaze. Now that I'm here and we're heading back to our room, I almost wish we weren't. The sooner we get back, the sooner we have this night—and the sooner she runs back to Jake.

Maybe I shouldn't do this with her. I know myself better than anyone else does, and once I have her, I won't be able to stay away. Bet hell, if I turn her down again, like I did at the retreat, I'd hate myself more than she would.

She taps the app on her phone and holds it to the door to unlock it. She moves inside the room slowly, and yes, I'm watching her every move. When she gazes over her shoulder and nods, I don't think twice about joining her.

She leans up against the wall, and the look she gives me, the one that tells me she wants me just as much as I want her, spurs me to close the gap.

My lips press against hers. I reach down to grab her perfectly plump ass and wrap her legs around me.

She moans, wrapping her arms around neck. The simple noise hits me right in the chest, and I swear I can't even remember a time that existed before Willa.

"I have a confession to make," she says, pulling back. I miss her lips already, and I don't care how cheesy I sound. I'll never get tired of kissing Willa.

"What's that?"

"Do you remember that sex scene you asked me to read when we were on the retreat?"

How could I ever forget?

"Yes."

She draws small circles on my chest as she thinks over her words. "Well, I never actually read the entire thing."

"What?"

"I sort of … got distracted with thinking about you being that guy and me being that woman and I went to this place—"

"You imagined me and you against the wall, didn't you?"

Her cheeks blush.

"I knew it."

I capture her mouth with my own, plunging my tongue between her lips.

"If you want to know how the scene ended, I'll show you."

"I almost skimmed through one of your other books to find a steamy scene," she says as I trail kisses down her neck and between her breasts, moving us to the bed, where I climb over her. "But I didn't know how much more it would make me want you, and not knowing what was going to happen between us, I just couldn't bring myself to do it."

"Baby, I'll show you exactly what I've imagined in every single book and every single intimate scene." I pull back to look into her eyes. "I've written a lot of books."

Her nose wrinkles as she smiles. "Good."

"But the scenes I've written since I've met you are one of a kind."

"So, you've imagined this?"

"Imagined this? Hell, Willa, I've played this out in my head every single night since the retreat."

With more strength than I gave her credit for, she grabs a leg at my hip and rolls us until she's on top.

Oh hell. My heart is pounding, and my dick is getting harder than a rock and we still have our clothes on.

"What if I play out the next scene I want you to write?"

Ooo-kay, Zane, don't choke on your own spit.

"You, uh, you want me to write out, uh, what we do?"

She shrugs and then starts to unbuckle my pants. "Would that be weird?"

"Would it be weird to let millions of readers read a scene that you and I have actually done?"

"And no one would know but us."

Fuck. Me.

My entire body is frozen as I stare at the unpredictable woman smiling down at me. Yeah, it's official: this one night isn't going to be enough for me.

"Was that too much? You're just staring at me now, and earlier you were all Mr. Dirty Talker, so I was trying to match your energy. Maybe I took it too far."

Still, I don't say anything. I can't. This woman was made for me.

"Okay," she says and starts to crawl off me.

"Tell me to take my clothes off," I say, stopping her and holding her in place as I lift my hips, so she knows what she's done to me.

Her gaze flicks to where we're connected and then back to my eyes.

"Say it."

"Take your clothes off," she says and then smiles a slow, wicked smile. "Now."

She doesn't have to ask me twice. I strip underneath her and never let my eyes stray from hers, even when I lift her to balance on her knees while I slide off my pants. When all that's left are my boxers, I reach for her clothes.

"If I'm naked, you're naked."

"Yes, sir."

I growl and strip her down until only her bra and thong remain.

No one has ever called me sir before, not before or during sex. I could get on board with it.

One look at her and I decide that I need it all gone. I lift her up, slap her ass, and then rip her panties off.

She squeals and unclips her bra, dropping back on the bed and scooting toward the headboard.

"Maybe we can act out that scene next time. Right now, I just need you."

Her confession sends my already-hard cock springing to attention.

"Whatever you want, baby, you got it."

Her chest raises and lowers in deep breaths as I settle myself over her. I kiss her lips, her neck, her chest, and make my way down until I kiss her right between the legs.

"Oh, Zane," she moans.

My name on her lips sends me into a frenzy. I lick her entire core and then slip a finger in. Her back arches off the bed, and she clenches the sheets with her hands.

"All that from just a finger," I say and then lick her once more. This time, I don't stop. I lick faster and faster, occasionally slipping a finger in to work her up.

Her breathing is fast, and I can feel the grip around my fingers just before she cries out.

"Holy hell, Zane!"

I don't give her enough time to come down before I'm on her, tearing open the condom wrapper I'd pulled from my wallet before we started and sliding it on.

I plunge into her in one fast, hard thrust.

"Yes! Oh my god, yes!"

I pull back and slowly reenter her tight-as-sin pussy.

"Shit, Willa. Shit!" I say and pause. "You're so fucking tight."

"That's a line from a book, isn't it?" she breathes, running a hand through her hair.

"Maybe, but I never knew what the hell it meant till just now."

She laughs and I kiss the addictive sound right off her lips before slamming into her again.

I pick up the pace, following her greedy orders of *faster* and *harder,* and just like that, I've never wanted to please someone as much as I want to please her. Hell, her orders are turning me on even more, and if I can't ignite orgasm two soon, I'm going to look like a preteen kid who can't control himself.

"Yes! Right there, don't stop, don't—oh! I'm … I'm …"

"Willa," I say as my orgasm runs through my veins the second her body pulses around me.

Slowly, we come back to reality, and I move off her.

"I had no idea you'd—"

"It's been a long time."

"How fucking—?"

"More than a year."

"A year is way—"

"Too long. I know."

"Are you going to let me finish even one sentence?"

"I don't know how to have manners right now. I have no idea what just happened. I can't even see straight."

I chuckle and pull her into my chest, kissing her shoulder.

Now that I think about it, one weekend is better than one

night. Yeah, after this weekend, I have no idea how I'll let her go, but I will because Willa deserves someone who is fully devoted to her. Someone who can give her the world and love her the way she deserves to be loved.

That person is not a romance writer who has no idea how to accept and be in love with himself.

CHAPTER TWENTY
WILLA

If I hadn't fallen for Zane yet, this wedding and weekend were bound to push me over the edge. Especially watching him dance with his mom right now. He is truly not the man I expected after that first night we spoke at the bar. Ha. The night he called me out for failing miserably to get Jake's attention.

A smile touches my lips. So much has changed in such a short amount of time.

I look around the room as music fills the background. His brother and his new wife chose a sleek black, white, and gold wedding theme, and everything about the decor is classy. Simple vases for the centerpieces, gold chairs with white seats and white tablecloths. The seating wasn't assigned, which Zane loved because he isn't forced to sit with his family and make small talk. It means we get to sit with his friends. I should say our friends, really, because even after this weekend, there is no way I couldn't not see them again.

After this weekend.

After.

What do we do after?

I don't want to go back to being strangers, and yet he told me right from the start that he doesn't do relationships.

But last night.

Hell, last night.

The sex.

Wow.

It …

I …

Wow.

"How long have you two been dating?" a soft voice asks behind me. I twist to face the woman and see white. Lots of white.

The bride grabs the train of her dress, sweeps it to her side; and sits next to me. Immediately, I look around for Zane. Or any of those so-called friends I was just thinking about.

I don't spot a single one of them.

"Me?" I ask.

She laughs as if I'm the funniest person in the world.

"Yeah, you. I'm Mandy."

She offers me her hand, and even knowing the circumstance that brought me here, this is still her wedding, so I take it and smile. "Willa."

"Oh my gosh, that's beautiful."

"Thank you."

"So give me all the details for you and my brother-in-law."

I hesitate, and she reads me instantly.

"He told you, didn't he?"

I nod. No further explanation needed.

"You must think I'm a horrible person. Oh god, and what you must think of his brother."

That they both suck a little, yeah, but I'm not about to tell her that.

She sighs and grabs a flute of champagne offered to her. She takes one for me, too, and then clinks my glass. I drink half the glass while she barely takes a sip.

This is odd, but I really have no idea what to do from here.

"Have you ever had a plan?" she asks me.

"A plan for what?"

"Life, love, anything really."

Oddly enough, my entire love life these days is only because of a plan.

I nod.

"Me too. I thought I had it all figured out and that everything I had in my plan couldn't get any better. I just had to stick to it."

A little smile touches my lips because her story matches mine more than she knows.

"But then you meet the one person who just," she shakes her head, "excuse the language, fucks that plan up. Who shows up and rewrites the entire thing for you, and they write it better than you even thought it could ever be written. There is this pull toward them, and you know that as long as you have that person, you can face anything this world offers you."

It's no guess that Zane's brother is this person for her.

"Have you ever had that?"

"A plan or the person who wrecks my well-thought-out plans?"

"Both."

"Well," I began, then Zane steps back into the banquet room. His eyes find mine immediately, and the last couple of weeks flash through my mind. I did have a plan, then I met Zane.

"Yes."

"So you get it then? I didn't want to hurt Zane. God, neither of us did, but we just … you get it, right?"

I could go on and on about how no matter what happened with Zeke, Zane deserved better. He deserved to know sooner, and he deserved for her to break it off before she fooled around with his brother. Yet I don't say any of those things. The past is the past, and I can't change it for Zane. I can, however, change his future.

I know he said he doesn't do relationships or commitment. I get it more than he knows now, but I can't let him lose out on something spectacular because he's scared.

Zane and I could be amazing together.

If only …

If only times were different. If only he didn't have a broken heart that he thinks doesn't deserve mending, and if only I weren't leaving. I don't have the job yet, but I'm pretty sure it's mine. What Zane and I have has a time limit, and we both know it.

The rest of the night falls into a blur of dancing and drinks, so soon enough, we are headed up the elevator.

"Did you have fun tonight?" Zane asks as we reach the room.

"I did."

He spins me around, helping me with the zipper at the back of my dress. I feel the soft touch of his knuckles all the way down my back. He smooths his hands up my spine to my shoulder and drops the dress at my feet.

"Fuck. You are stunning, Willa."

I take a breath as his lips touch the back of my neck. It's the first time anyone has ever kissed me there, and it's amazing. My nipples harden instantly, and I never want him to stop kissing me. Something about not being able to see what he's going to do next turns me on more than I thought it would. A finger tickles my sides, slowly moving down to my hip.

"Willa, the things I want to do you are insane, but I can't do them knowing I could be leading you on."

"Leading me on how?"

"Because you want love and commitment, and I can't give you those things."

"I'm aware of that."

"And you still want this?"

I nod.

"I'm happy, Zane, for the first time in a long time. You've shown me what it's like to be with someone who appreciates what they have, and I just … I don't want to let that go just yet. Whatever you want to give me, I want to take."

He moves in front of me and studies my eyes for a moment before nodding.

"Okay, I want these off," he says and tugs at the string of my underwear.

I nod quickly and move to do as he demanded, but he stops me.

"Don't you dare take this moment from me," he says with a raspy tone as he drops to his knees.

There was a moment during the evening when I was

convinced that last night was a one-time thing for this week-end, but wow, am I glad that I was wrong.

He hooks his fingers into the string of my thong and tugs it down my legs. I step out of it, and then he dips his head between my parted legs.

"I've never tasted anyone as sweet as you, Willa. I've been thinking about this all night. When they said the cake was to die for, I wanted to tell them that clearly, they've never gone down on you."

I let out a squeak at the idea of him confessing that in front of the bride or groom.

Zane pauses after one lick and looks up at me. "Is something funny?"

The sight of him on his knees, still in his suit, makes me weak. I lift one leg to his shoulder before I answer.

"I was just imagining if you had actually said that. I would have been mortified, but I think we could have left a lot sooner."

A sinful smirk takes over his lips. "I'll remember that for next time."

Then he plunges his tongue against me, and I buckle, grip-ping his head for support. He doesn't take it easy on me—no, his tongue digs into me and his fingers press against my clit, causing my body to erupt into darkness within seconds.

I'm still coming down when he picks me up and tosses me on the bed. I touch myself because I don't want this feeling to end. When I open my eyes, Zane is in front of me, completely naked, with his hard erection in his hand.

"Don't stop," he says, his gaze fixed on where my hand is pressing between my legs.

"I'd rather this was you."

"Fuck, baby, so do I, but watching you teach me is bringing my cock to a whole new level of hard."

I roll my head back and groan. "Get over here."

I don't care if sex between us goes fast. I just want him and the way he makes me feel, and the sooner we make that happen, the sooner we can do it again.

I feel him crawl onto the bed, but instead of moving on top of me, he lies next to me.

I turn my head and our gazes lock.

"What do you want?" he asks me.

"I want you inside me."

Holy shit, I just said that. I didn't know I was a dirty talker until I met Zane.

Clearly, I just needed the right guy.

"How do you want it?"

Instead of answering him, I straddle his lap, grabbing him and placing him at my entrance.

He grins and settles his hands on thighs. "Take it."

I want to go slow, I do, but I can't. I slide down in one swift motion, and this time, it's him who closes his eyes and rolls his head back into the pillow.

Watching his response is all the motivation I need to let myself lose control. I roll my hips forward and back and then in a circle. His eyes are still closed, and his grip on my legs tightens.

"Fuck, baby, that feels so good."

"I want you to come for me."

He grins, eyes still pinched shut. "That's my line."

I lean back, the pressure building quickly.

In a swift move, Zane grabs my hips and sits up, jerking

me back so that he can lean against the headboard, and then he pushes me away only to pull me back in another jerk.

He does that over and over, and the pressure shatters through my entire body, my vision blurring and my mouth opening, but no words come out.

"Holy fuck," Zane says, his body stilling underneath me. "Holy fuck."

He says it once more as he drops back, resting his head against the headboard and opening his eyes.

My eyes are locked on him in an instant, and I smile before leaning forward to kiss him.

The moment is broken by the sound of my phone going off. Zane wouldn't know it, but it's only a text. Yet given the consistent noise of someone clearly texting me over and over, you'd think it was ringing.

With one more kiss, he says, "Go ahead and get that. I'm going to get cleaned up and get you a towel."

Reluctantly, I climb off him and watch his bare backside as he retreats to the bathroom.

I can't help but smile. Again. I feel like that's all I've done the last two days. I don't even care how sappy I look. This weekend has been more than perfect.

My phone goes off again, so I roll to my side of the bed and grab it from my purse.

It's from Jake.

Jake: Rumor mill is that they are choosing San Fran leaders by the end of next week.

Jake: Rumor also has it that it's you and me.

Jake: Can you believe it?

Jake: It's happening. We are getting everything we want!

The happiness that was just coursing through my veins comes to a halt.

I hear the sink turn on.

Like I said, I knew we had a time limit, but I just met the perfect guy and now … I just leave?

CHAPTER TWENTY-ONE
ZANE

This is good.

This is how things are meant to be. Me back in my home office sitting in front of the computer, and Willa … not here.

Not around.

At her place. Not at mine.

Jesus, listen to me. How many ways can I say it before I can convince myself that not being near her is how it should be?

I scrub a hand over my face and groan.

Yeah, this is right.

I glance at the clock. It's almost five. It's Monday. I bet she's been with stupid Jake all day and they've been having a grand ole time laughing together.

Technically, he still thinks we've been broken up since before my brother's wedding, so I'm sure he's moving in quickly for date number two.

My gaze flashes to the document in front of me.

I never did ask her about their first date. If it was everything she dreamed of.

I was too caught up in being around her, and her presence clouded my judgment. I'm meant to be alone. To share meaningless hookups that leave zero people with heartbreak.

Not telling Willa how I feel was definitely the right choice. Zero heartbreak. Just how I like it.

You know what might help? If I put myself back into a routine.

It's not the weekend, but it's as good a night as any to start.

I pack up my laptop bag and head out the door.

Weeknights are slow at the bar, and there is a total of three people here when I walk in. This is good. I won't have to worry about being hit on, and I can get work done. Get my mind back in the game of what my life should be like.

I order a wheat beer on tap and pop open my computer.

With where my head is, unable to focus on anything specific right now, just opening a Word doc and writing whatever comes to mind is my best option. Just let the words flow.

I'm two pages in when the door opens.

"Oh my gosh, is that—?" a voice says behind me, followed by an overexaggerated squeal.

"It's Zane Rosey. *The* Zane Rosey."

I drop my head with a chuckle, and at the same time my heart swells.

Willa Boston.

I dropped her off yesterday fully intending on never seeing her again.

I should turn around and tell her to leave because the two of us make zero sense, but I can't. I can't even control myself.

Instead, I spin around, stand, and hook an arm around her waist, tugging her close to me.

"Oh wow," she laughs. "I missed you too."

I press my lips to hers and dig my hand into her backside.

Hell, kissing her should be a sin.

"You shouldn't be here," I tell her between kisses.

"I couldn't stay away."

Our gazes lock together, and I kiss her forehead. I feel the same way.

"Can I get you a drink?" I ask and she nods, placing her order. "How did you know I'd be here? Just taking a chance or what?"

"Are you kidding me? I knew you'd want to find a way to nix me from your system as fast as possible. Obviously, this is where you'd come. I wasn't shocked to walk in here and see that you weren't even trying. You were only killing time."

I keep my gaze on her and smirk. How does she know me that well after just a couple of weeks?

"So, does your visit tonight have a purpose?" I ask.

"It might."

"Willa, you know I can't—"

"I'm not asking you to date me. Zane, I can't seem to stay away from you, and I have a feeling you feel the same. Am I right?"

I sip my drink.

"You're not wrong."

"You don't date and there is a very good chance I'm leaving in a couple of months at most, so let's just have some fun till then, yeah? I think we both know how much fun we can have."

My cock hardens at just the thought of said fun. Of her

beneath me, on top of me, next to me. To the things that I could be doing to her right now.

"What happened to Jake?" I ask. "Last I heard, you two went on a date."

Her nose wrinkles.

"Yeah, and I told him I wasn't ready to date someone new and went to your house to invite myself to your brother's wedding."

I almost spit out my drink.

"It was bad?"

She groans and lays her head in her arms on the bar top. "He wasn't what I expected, and I blame you." She sits up quickly and slaps my arm. "You set the bar too high as a fake boyfriend on the retreat."

"Why didn't you tell me?"

She shrugs. "Like I said, you set the bar pretty high."

I chuckle a little and rub her back. "I'm sorry, Willa."

It's the only word I get out because the simple gesture of my hand touching her spikes the sexual tension between us and our gazes lock.

"I should probably tell you that I saw you on your date."

"Are you serious? Why did you act like you didn't know?"

I shrug. "I guess I wanted you to tell me on your own."

Her mouth twists. "I should have."

"And I should have told you that I saw you."

"Well, hey, look at us. Holding a grown-up conversation and making grown-up decisions."

I chuckle.

Perhaps Willa is onto something. A fling before she leaves. If we know the rules, we are always honest with each other, we can't get hurt, right? It makes sense—she knows I can't give her commitment and we both get great sex. She'll move in what, a month or two? That's plenty of time to get her out of my system.

"If we do this, Willa … I'm shit at relationships. You know this. I can't even promise that I'll be good at exclusive casualness."

Is that what this is called?

"I know." She shakes her head. "But not even putting the option on the table feels wrong."

She bites her bottom lip, and I know there is no way I can tell her no.

"All right. Deal."

She beams a smile. "Do we shake on it?"

I laugh. "We can grab a drink and then head back to my place."

"God, yes," she breathes.

Her words bring back memories of the weekend and instantly have to adjust myself.

"I have a signing the rest of the week, but this weekend, do you want to do something fun?"

She smirks.

"Okay, something clean and fun. We can do the dirty fun later."

"Ah, well, of course. If you're there, I'm there."

The pure happiness I feel sprinting through my body makes my heart race. It's been a long time since I let a woman in like this.

I'm not so sure I can handle it.

CHAPTER TWENTY-TWO

WILLA

I've been dying for some girl time, so the moment I spot Calla pull up and get out of her car, I swing the door open.

"I have so much to tell you."

She squeals, carrying a bottle of wine tucked under her arm and a bag of Oreos in the other. I invited Greer, too, but she couldn't make it. Something with her boyfriend or ex-boyfriend. I really need to find out what her story is.

"Yes," Calla cheers. "Oh my gosh, yes. I knew that trip would be good for you, and even though I was there, don't leave out any details."

She rushes into the kitchen, twists the top off the bottle—my favorite wine is the kind that doesn't take a lot of effort—and hands me the bottle.

"Okay, let's get to it. Now tell me how—"

"We slept together," I blurt out. "It was good. More than good. It was so amazing."

"Ah!" she screams, and I wave my hands, telling her to be quiet. "Oh my god, Willa."

"I know."

"So where does this leave the two of you?" She takes a cookie from its sleeve and leans into the couch.

I copy her and shrug. "Friend with benefits."

Her face wrinkles in disgust.

"Is that where you want it to leave you?"

"He made it clear he didn't want a relationship, and I'm basically moving soon, so I'm in for casualness."

"Eww."

I laugh.

She pauses and looks around. "Where is he now?"

"Not here," I laugh.

"No, I know that, but is he planning on coming over at all today? We should make a plan to change his mind."

I shake my head. "He had a signing in Denver today, and there will be no mind changing."

"Oh!" She palms her forehead. "I knew that. Beck wouldn't shut up about it over the weekend. How could I forget?"

Calla makes a fake gag face.

"Do you want to tell me about you and Beck?"

"Me and Beck? There is no me and Beck."

"Yeah, but what's your story? Why don't you like him? Isn't he from Melody like you?"

"I know he is. His sister is super sweet, but Beck is … not like her at all."

I switch out my cookie and grab my glass, taking a sip before I ask, "So why don't you like Beck? It's pretty clear you don't."

Her head bounces side to side. "I'd rather not talk about it."

"No way. Explain."

"It's really nothing. He was just Mr. Popular in school and probably didn't even notice me."

"Oh my gosh, Calla! Did you have a crush on Beck Robertson growing up?"

"No! Absolutely not." Her cheeks flush. "He just was that guy, you know, the one every girl wanted. He was a walking cliché in any '90s teen movie."

"Sure."

"He was."

I hold my hands up. "I'll take your word for it."

"Good. Now, back to you and Zane."

I smile. I can't help it.

"When will you see him next?"

"In a couple of days."

"Has he texted you since he's been gone?"

I nod. "Just small things to let me know they made it."

"You two are totally dating."

I shake my head.

"We aren't. We are being smart. I mean, I'm trying to get a job that's going to transfer me across the country. Getting into a relationship would be silly."

"Um, yeah, that's why this is perfect. The right guy always comes along at the worst time. Love doesn't come with a warning, babe. Face it, you're dating."

"We aren't."

She sighs heavily then changes the subject, which I'm glad about. I was eager to tell her about Zane, but a part of what she said is right. We are basically dating. What happens when I get this job? When will I leave?

It doesn't matter. I know what this is. He knows what this is. That's that.

Still, I wonder if he's thinking of me the way I'm thinking of him right now.

I miss the guy, and it hasn't even been a whole day since I saw him last.

Shit.

Maybe this wasn't the brightest idea. Then again, maybe it was. Maybe this time will show him that he can be good, even great, at relationships.

My heart hammers in my chest. And if he doesn't see that …

It's a risk I'm willing to take.

* * *

Turns out, I don't have to wait two days to see where Zane's mind is, because at 9:30 p.m., while I have a face mask the color of green poop on my face, he attempts to FaceTime.

I practically yelp when I see his name, ignoring the call and tossing my phone onto the bed face down.

My watch buzzes with a notification.

Zane: Answer your phone *wink emoji*
  Willa: Can't. Busy.
  Zane: Oh yeah, doing what? Reading one of my books?

I smirk and sit on the bed, settling against my headboard to text him back.

. . .

Willa: Yes, and I'm super deep into this scene while you're bothering me.

    Zane: Which scene?

    Willa: A steamy one.

    Zane: Tell me the book and page number.

I hesitate to text back.

Willa: Guess.

    Zane: If you're that into it, I'm going with *The Big Man on Campus* and page ninety-two on the e-book.

I log into my online reader, buy the book super-fast, and find the page he's referring to. I read the first line.

Lie back and spread your legs.

I flip my e-reader face down. He would. When I don't answer right away, he attempts to call me again.

    I groan, stepping into the bathroom to wash off my face. When I finish, I see that I missed his call again.

Zane: Willa …

Zane: Did you go look up the page I just mentioned?
Willa: No.

And another FaceTime.

I answer it right away.

"Wow, someone misses me." I grin into the phone, my breath hitching when I see him lying on the hotel bed shirtless.

"Damn right I did. I haven't stopping thinking about you since I left."

"Oh."

"Don't tell me you didn't know that."

"I didn't."

"Willa," he says, adjusting to get fully into the screen. "Now that I've had a taste of you, there is no way you're getting rid of me. As soon as I get back, we are recreating our weekend away, and I'm not letting you out of my sight."

Okay, yeah, I'm pretty sure he could count every single one of my teeth with the way I'm smiling. Also, I guess that answers my question about where his head is at with us.

"I can handle that," I say and lay on my bed too. "Why didn't you go out with the guys?"

"I had something more important I wanted to do."

God, his cheeky grin can make any girl blush, and right now, that grin just so happens to be pointed at me.

"What's that?" I ask and slowly push the side of my robe off my shoulder.

His growl hits me right between the legs.

"Well, it was talking to you, but if you were hinting at something else, I could be persuaded."

"Good."

He shakes his head. "Open that book we were just talking about and turn to that same page."

Since I'd only just set the e-reader on my bed, I reach for it and then settle back into position.

"Willa, babe, are you reading naughty books in bed?"

I palm my forehead.

"No. Oh my gosh, Zane, I'm not sure I can do this. I feel weird."

"Weird? Baby, I'm about to make you feel good, and I'm not even there."

I laugh. "Whoa, that's a line if I ever heard one."

"Willa!"

"Sorry, okay." I put on a serious face and look into the camera. "What do you want me to do next?"

"I want you to read the first line of the book to yourself and do just as it says."

All right, let it be known that I'll never be able to read another one of his books the same way again.

CHAPTER TWENTY-THREE
ZANE

Willa Boston.

Damn.

This woman is definitely a new addiction.

I hate that as soon as we got back from the wedding, I had to head to Denver for a book signing.

Thank god for FaceTime.

And boy, did I get the best FaceTime of my life. I'll never look at that bright green button again without thinking of Willa on the other end of it.

Who would have thought? Me. In a relationship … of sorts. Hell, me at my brother's wedding. It's safe to say that this summer, although not over yet, has been life changing.

After the breakup, I honestly thought I'd never find someone who challenged me enough or made me feel like as long as we were together, we could accomplish anything. Willa does that. She reminds me that there is a playful side of me that hasn't been out in a while. A side of me that doesn't balk at every little thing around me or turn every fun event into a grumpy one.

A great example is Tobias's annual barbeque. I wasn't sure he was actually going to have it. His birthday was a month ago, and he once mentioned how much he likes to celebrate before book tour season. Not this year. Although, to be honest, Doug, our agent, did tours differently this year, and they are so sporadic that we will be holding signings through September.

Anyway, each year, there is a game involved with the night, and this year, I'm not rolling my eyes at the thought. Nope. I have my girl on my arm and a smile on my face.

It's not lost on me how good things have been with me and Willa or how I don't overthink every little detail between us or how easy it is to just let myself be happy. I like this new me. Even if it's only temporary. Which, I'm pretty certain, is the only reason things are the way they are. I know when and how this will end. It won't be a shock to me, so I can't be heartbroken when it's over. Maybe the peace of mind of knowing the ending is all I need.

We get out of my car, and "Black Betty" is blaring from Tobias's backyard. Everyone is probably already out there, so I choose to take us through the side gate instead of through the house to get to the party.

The spring on the gate is tighter than I remember, so when it slams shut, it draws attention to us, and Willa and I freeze.

Like our writing session when everyone discovered I had feelings for Willa, everyone falls silent.

Now, I know I'm stepping outside of my box here, but this is ridiculous. Were they not expecting me to bring her? To not keep seeing her after everything I admitted to them?

"Is it just me or are they all staring super weird-like?"

I clear my throat and do a little hand gesture that Willa can see to tell them all to turn around. "It's not you. It's them."

"Oh, okay, why are they staring?"

I sigh. I may as well be honest. When it comes to Willa, I always am. Can't stop now. "We've been having barbecues for years as a group, and this is the first time I've ever brought someone with me."

Willa chuckles.

"Dang, Rosey." Tobias shouts from his seat near the grill. "You really are just living life on the wild side this summer, aren't you? Wellness retreats with a stranger, weddings with a fake girlfriend whom you decided to make a real one, and now showing up to an event with your friends with said real girlfriend. What are you going to do next? Push her against the side of my house and strip her clothes off?"

I groan. "It's not the worst option," I say loud enough for only Willa to hear.

I don't bother correcting him that Willa isn't my real girlfriend.

Willa laughs and then pushes my arm away as she walks toward the group. "Well, come on."

I take two long strides to catch up. "Do people really think I haven't done crazier things than fake dating a girl or attending weddings and retreats?"

She shakes her head. "Well, from what I know and clearly what your friends know, you have an image that you don't typically break character from. You're an honest person. Too honest maybe, and them seeing you change your ways because you met me is pretty crazy."

"You make it sound like I was a grump."

"Weren't you?" she asks and then smiles at Tobias. "Hi, I'm Willa."

"Tobias. It's good to finally meet you. That's Natalie," he says, and the smile he gives his "best friend" looks a lot like the one I give Willa.

"Hi." Natalie beams and then looks at me, her smile growing bigger. "Calla and Greer have told me pretty good things about you."

"Yikes," Willa laughs. "Just pretty good?"

"I've been waiting for you," Calla says, stepping out of the house. Nora is right behind her.

"Me too. Natalie, come with us," Greer adds, waving them in.

Natalie says something to Willa as they head to the house, but I don't hear it.

Instead, I drop to the chair between Simon and Beck, and Tobias hands me a beer.

"That's her, huh?" he asks, sitting across from me. Everyone is here. Graham and Hero included, but they are over by the cornhole boards with Simon's son, Grey.

"That's her."

"I'm happy for you, man." He clinks his beer to mine.

"I'm happy, too, but hey—not that I'm complaining because I like that Willa has someone around that she knows—but is Calla going to be like a staple to our group?"

Simon nods. "Probably. Greer, too, it seems. She and Calla have been hanging out a lot."

I flash a glance at Beck, who remains focused on the mouth of his beer. Without looking at anyone or making a sound, he chugs the rest of it.

"Anyone want another?" he asks, but he gets up and moves to the house before we answer.

"What's his problem?" I ask.

"Besides the fact that my sister is making his days hell when she is around, nothing. He did mention his struggle with a novel. The ending of his current project isn't coming together."

"Ah." I nod. He'll be distracted for weeks if he doesn't figure it out. "Let's put it at the top of our list for this week. We won't write until he has something solid."

My friends nod in agreement and then disperse around the yard. Simon heads for the cornhole boards, and Tobias and Graham go for horseshoes. I hear the faint sound of laughter from the house and smile to myself.

The summer of Willa Boston is going to be one I will never forget.

CHAPTER TWENTY-FOUR
WILLA

Group gatherings are probably one of my favorite things in the entire world. Especially with Zane's friends.

Holy moly, how have I not been having this much fun over burgers and beers?

We have successfully won three rounds of cornhole, one round of horseshoes—absolutely pure beginner's luck, because what even is that game? —and two rounds of flip cup. To which we played with water because Grey wanted to play.

Now we've just cracked open a couple of beers and Zane is huddled into me as we watch the others group up in front of us.

"What's happening now?" I ask, leaning into Zane. His spicy scent sends a tingle through my body. I could never tell him this, but just the smell of him makes me feel alive. It makes me happy, and it makes me look forward to a future I didn't know I wanted till he came along.

"Another game."

"Another?" I ask, faking shock with my hand on my heart. "I had no idea."

He nods and turns to me. Our lips are just a whisper away from brushing. His gaze drops to mine before flashing back to my eyes. I swear he just hitched his breath.

I'm the first to move. I don't go far. Maybe a half step back. We don't have to be all over each other all the time.

Zane takes this moment to widen his stance, cross his arms, and lean toward me.

"Well, as you can tell, we like competition. I think it makes up for the lack of it that we have toward our books. In that aspect, we are all about support, so we had to find one way to show we are better than each other. It sounds dumb, but we have a blast. Anyway, during at least one barbeque of the year, like this afternoon, we have a tournament between our little group. The winner gets to dictate a book title to each loser, and the writers must use what he assigned them for a manuscript during the next year."

"That's what we've been playing for this entire time?" I ask. I just thought we were having fun.

A flash of Tobias bumping and elbowing Hero during cup flip makes sense now.

"Yes, and we are tied with Beck. I'm not letting him win."

"Oh, this sounds risky."

He nods. "It is."

"So, how many books have they named for you?"

Zane's thick laugh hits me in the core. "I hope I never find out."

"Is everyone ready?"

"Ready?" I gulp. "I don't even know what we are doing."

"This one is easy. At the start of the party, we each hide

two of our own books throughout the yard. You get a point for each book you find."

"Huh, so an Easter egg hunt."

"Pretty much."

"All right. I'm ready."

Tobias clicks his thumb on the timer in his hand. It reminds me of the stopwatch my gym teacher in elementary school used.

"Ten seconds," he announces, and my heart starts to race.

I feel like a kid.

The timer buzzes and everyone scatters.

As soon as we take off, Zane grabs my hand, basically dragging me with him. "Hurry, this way. I know where at least four books are."

"Have you been looking for them all night? Isn't that cheating?"

"No. Never. Work smarter, not harder, right?"

I barely keep up with him as we round the side of the house. Hero and his fiancée come barreling toward us. Zane reacts first, hand on my hip to move me out of the way. The four of us won't fit on the side of the house, so he turns to flatten himself against me as the other two pass.

The moment they're gone, I expect him to move. After all, he was pretty pumped just seconds ago to win this thing, but right now, it doesn't look like he wants to go anywhere.

His nose brushes against mine.

I suck in a breath, and he growls.

"Willa."

God, just hearing him say my name perks my nipples up. The hand that was on my hip tickles its way to my belly button. I grip his shirt and pull him closer.

We've been finding ourselves in situations like this more and more lately. I have no doubt that this moment is going to be the one that breaks us.

I'm not mad.

I'm eager.

I'm here for it.

"If we don't move, we are going to lose," I whisper, my upper lip brushing against his lower one.

"I know."

He brushes his lips over mine and then hovers.

"Say something." I cup the side of his face and wait.

"Baby, you don't want to know the things I want to say to you right now."

With my heart pounding, I say, "Maybe I do."

"How quiet can you be?" he asks. I adjust the way I'm standing so that he has one leg between mine as he keeps me pinned against the house.

"Let's find out," I answer.

I expect him to kiss me, but instead of touching his lips to mine, he dips to kiss my neck, peppering more kissing down my chest. His hand slides down my hip to my maxi skirt and slowly begins to bunch it bit by bit until my bare leg breaks free. There isn't a slit in this skirt, so if one side is bunched up, both sides are.

Slowly, painfully slowly, he continues kissing my chest as he holds my right leg up, bent at his waist. His other hand tickles up the inside of my thigh until he reaches my panties, and he doesn't hesitate before he moves them to the side and slides a finger in.

"Damn, Willa, how long have you been this wet?"

"Basically since you picked me up."

His forehead drops to my shoulder.

"Fuck, you can't say things like that."

"Oh, but you can."

He chuckles and then kisses me.

"Just one big relationship of sexual torture, huh?"

"If it works, it works."

He steals another kiss, adding a finger to the other between my legs, and he keeps kissing me right on through the gasp that wants to escape me.

He slides in and out and flicks and curls his fingers inside me until the only way to keep silent is for me to bite his shoulder.

"Oh my god," I whisper as he adjusts my clothing. "Did that really just happen?"

He chuckles. "It did."

"We better get back before someone comes looking for us."

He spins, leans against the house, and pulls me against him for a kiss.

"Would that be so bad?"

"Yes," I say with a laugh and push him off. "Now, let's go, and keep your hands to yourself."

"Ugh, that's the worst. All I want to do is touch you."

"Clearly."

With his hand in mine, we round the side of the house toward the entire group that's back on the patio. I can't speak for Zane, but the way we are together doesn't feel casual. I mean, heck, he brought me here with his friends. Maybe he does see what this could be with us.

I pinch my lips together to hide a giant smile and look up as we approach the others. Just like when we entered at the beginning of the party, everyone turns to look at us. This time, though, knowing smiles greet us. Well, all except for Beck. He steps forward and cheers while pointing at Zane.

"I get to name your next book!"

All the guys start to tease him about losing, and he leaves me to get another beer.

I can't remember a time when I was this happy.

I'm getting everything I ever wanted.

The problem is, if I truly do get the job in California, where does that leave me and Zane?

CHAPTER TWENTY-FIVE
ZANE

In the last week, Willa and I have grown into a comfortable routine. During the day, she works at the clinic, and I work on my writing. As soon as she's home, I meet her here and cook dinner while she does a little computer work. Then we eat, fool around, and go to bed. It's honestly so mundane, but I fucking love it.

With a belly full of fettuccine alfredo, Willa is still hard at work on her computer. She's got one foot propped up on her chair as she types. I smile. She's focused. I love that and her determination. She likes being good at what she does, and so do I. Having someone around who meets my energy—well, I didn't realize I needed it.

I didn't realize how much I needed *her*. I could be rushing it, and I know the deal we made, but hell, I don't ever want to go back to a life without her.

"Holy shit," she says and sits up. Her foot drops to the floor. "Holy shit."

"What's going on?" I ask. The expression on her face is clearly shock, but I can't tell if it's good or bad.

"I just got a job offer," she says. "For the San Fran location. It's a good one. Oh my god. I did it."

"Congratulations. That's amazing," is my initial reaction, but on the inside, my heart is ready to beat out of my chest.

I pull her in for a hug so she can't see my eyes. She's told me time and time again that she knows what I'm thinking with just a look. If that's true, I don't want her to know right now.

I just found her. I don't want to lose her.

I pull back, and the frown on her face confuses me. "Why don't you look excited?"

"I am excited."

"Oye, you sure don't sound excited."

She lets out a long breath. "If I take the job, I have to move."

I nod.

"To California."

"I know."

"What are you thinking?" she asks and reaches for my hand.

I force a smile. "That I'm proud of you. That you earned this, and I'm glad they see how perfect you are for the position."

"But?"

I shake my head. "But nothing."

"Should I take it?"

I groan and start to pack up my things. "That's not my choice."

She nods and then looks back at her computer.

"If you were me, what would you do?"

"I'm not answering that."

"Please."

"No."

"Zane, I really want to know your thoughts on this. Please talk to me."

"I don't want you to fucking leave, okay? I don't want you to leave. But you can't stay here because of me. You can't."

"Hey," she says, cupping my cheek with her hand until I look at her. "It's not official, okay? It's just an offer."

"But you want it." I step back out of her touch and put my hands on her hips. "You want to take it."

"I want to know it's an option."

He nods slowly. "You want options?"

"Yes."

"Fine. Here's one more."

Before she can take her next breath, I rush toward her, backing her up to the wall and slam my lips down on hers. My hands are in her hair and my hips are pressing into hers. A moan slips past her lips as her tongue tangles with mine.

All the air I have is sucked out of me, but I don't care. I'd give it all away if it meant I could keep kissing Willa.

She grabs my shirt, pulling me as close as she can get me. Our minds must think alike because I reach for her leg at the same time as she lifts it to hook around my waist.

I grind into her, my erection pressing against her stomach.

I've never wanted someone so much in my entire life. She reaches for the buckle on my jeans, but before she can do that, I break the kiss and step back.

We're both breathing heavily as we stare at each other.

"I have to go," I tell her before this goes too far.

I grab my coat off the back of the chair and head for the door.

"I will call you later," I say, and I leave.

She doesn't try to stop me.

I think she knows just as much as I do that if we keep this up and she stays, there will always be that bit in my mind that she will never know how San Francisco could have helped her career. Maybe she'll wonder too. But at the same time, if she chooses to leave, both our hearts will be broken.

So it's better to put some distance between us now than let this go too far.

The shitty thing is that my feelings for her were already there.

I need air, and I need to think. She said she wanted an option, but there really is only one. She has to take the job. She's been working for this position for years. Maybe not the exact one, but you don't work as hard as she does and not expect a promotion to come from it at some point.

This is where she's supposed to be in life.

And she's—oh fuck. *Fuck!* Who did they choose to go with her?

CHAPTER TWENTY-SIX
WILLA

I've given Zane three days to come around. Three days. That's seventy-two hours where we have exchanged only text messages. Seventy-two hours I haven't seen him.

And honestly, that's unacceptable.

Yeah, he needs time to think. Get some space.

I don't.

Either he wants to be with me, or he doesn't. And job offer or not, I deserve better than that.

I pull into Zane's driveway, and even though this is something I've done time after time again, today feels different.

I refuse to leave his house without knowing where we stand. I don't have it in me to keep wondering or overthinking. I want this with him. I want it all.

His front door swings open, and he jogs out as I'm getting out of my car.

He cups the right side of my face, kisses my forehead, and the tears I'd sworn I wasn't going to shed fall.

"Baby, hey, whoa. Tell me what's wrong. Did something happen?"

I shake my head, but quickly turn it into a nod.

Is he seriously going to act like nothing has changed between us over the last few days?

"Come on," he says, lacing his hand with mine and pulling me into his house. "This morning I baked you those cinnamon chocolate chips bars you like, with the almond flour and all. We can eat those, and you can tell me everything. I planned on bringing them to you later today."

Yep, clearly in his eyes, nothing has changed.

He pauses to look at me.

"I'm not an idiot. I know I'm responsible for some of those tears and it fucking kills me. I just, I'm not sure how to fix it."

He made me cookie bars?

He has to feel the same, right? He was going to come see me today to do what?

Now that I'm here, I have no idea what to say. I mean, I do, but how am I going to get the words out?

"Sit," he says, "I'll be right back."

He grabs the bars and a blackberry Hint water and returns to his living room where I'm sitting. When did he buy the Hint water? He said they were horrible, but he knows I—

"I fell for you," I blurt out.

Zane, who had been placing a bar on a napkin, freezes. He doesn't turn to look at me; he doesn't move a muscle.

I swallow. "You told me not to. I know you did. Well, not in so many words, but you told me that you don't date, and I get it. But things happened, obviously, and there is something here. You feel it too, don't you?"

He clears his throat and jumps up.

"Willa, why would you tell me that?"

Why? Why wouldn't I?

"Because I can't keep doing this. You and I both know we passed the point of pretending a long time ago."

"I thought we were just having fun," he says, and I swear it feels like I've been slapped.

"Fun?" I look at the food he baked me and at the way he hasn't let go of my hand. "This is fun for you?"

"You know what I mean. It was just casual."

"Casual?" I snap. My voice squeaks. "I'm pretty sure the way we have acted around everyone was more than just casual. The deal we made was stupid. We are way past casual, Zane."

I pinch my eyes closed. Why is he saying this? Why is he—?

"Are you saying this because of the job?"

He swallows hard and steps back, pulling his hand away from mine.

"Maybe you should go, Willa. Call Jake. Tell him we broke up and you need someone to talk to."

"No."

"That's how this was always supposed to go." His voice raises. "We should have been stricter with what we were doing. We got carried away. That's all."

"Is it?"

"Yes."

"It's not."

"Come on, Willa, go. Go find Jake. Find the guy this whole thing was intended for."

"I don't want Jake," I say as he yanks open the fridge to grab a beer. "I want you."

"You don't want me, Willa. You want a relationship, and I …"

"You what?"

"You can have that with Jake."

"Stop saying that!" I yell and hold my head high. I came here to say something, and I'll be damned if I'm going to let this conversation get in the way of that. "I'm only going to say this once, Zane Rosey. If you want to be with me, be with me. Right now. Tomorrow. The next day and every day after. If you don't, then you had better let me go when I walk out that door."

I can feel the tears pushing their way through, but I hold back. I will not let him see me cry. I know it's hard for him to accept that someone could want him. That someone could choose him. But I can't do this. He needs to make a choice. The longer he keeps this up, the worse both of us will get hurt.

I study him. The way he never takes his eyes off me. The way his chest rises and falls with every breath and the way his hands ball into fists at his side.

The look he's giving me says that he wants me to stay, but if he doesn't actually say the words, I can't keep standing here.

I nod. I've waited long enough. Time to head for the door.

This is it; Zane and I are—

"Stop."

Every part of me freezes except my heart. It's racing like a horse at the Kentucky Derby.

I feel him more than hear him as he approaches me.

His hands touch my shoulders first as he leans in to kiss my back.

"I … I can't let you go."

"Then don't," I say over my shoulder. "Don't."

"I might ruin this. I'm not good at it. I overthink a lot."

"You won't ruin anything," I say, turning to face him. I hold his face in my hands. "You have me, and I have you. We got this. Mistakes will happen, but as long as we're together, we'll get through them."

"You promise?"

"I promise." I push up to press my lips to his. He wastes no time reaching around to cup my butt and lift me. I wrap my legs around him and push the door closed.

The grown-up in me would cut this off so we can cover all the topics that need to be addressed. Especially the one we missed about my job offer, but I don't. Instead, we slowly peel each other's clothes off and show each other just how much we missed by being apart the last few days.

We tackled one problem today. The rest—well, it can wait till tomorrow. After all, I still don't know if I should take the job. Things are different now. If I'm being honest, I think the job was so appealing to me because it was a way to bring me and Jake together. I'd be the only person he knew, and he'd be forced to talk to me every single day. Now, it just seems silly to move to another state to keep doing exactly what I'm doing.

Wow.

I guess that's that.

I'm staying.

I'm staying, and Zane and I are going to give a real relationship a chance.

Zane, Zane. Zane. And here you thought you couldn't do the relationship thing.

From my eyes, he definitely can.

CHAPTER TWENTY-SEVEN
WILLA

The next morning when I get to work, Jake is waiting for me behind the front counter. He's been out of town since we were given our offers, and this will be the first time we've talked about it in person. Hopefully, he doesn't mention all the calls I didn't answer.

He has a coffee in each hand. Just at a quick glance, I can see that he didn't make me a coffee in the break room. He intentionally went out of his way to get one for me.

"Good morning, Willa. How are you today?" He beams a smile and rounds the counter, his arms stretched out as I eye the cup.

"What's this for?"

"It's a celebratory coffee."

"For?"

"For the fact that they chose you and me to run the office in Cali. Aren't you happy?"

I nod, reading the sticker on my cup. Black with a splash of cream. Vomit. Is he for real? We have made coffee in the same break room for years. Years. I really was blind when it came to him. Zane knew my coffee order within two days.

Just thinking about him makes me smile.

"I knew you'd see it the way I do."

"What?" I ask, sipping the crappy coffee and holding in a cringe. I need creamer. Stat.

"We should leave as early as possible. I'm thinking like a month before the opening. Since they are taking care of everything and—"

"I'm not going to take it," I cut him off.

It's a dream come true, yes, but Zane … he's an unexpected part of my life that I want just as much as this job. Don't get me wrong, knowing they chose me made my day, but Zane, he makes so much more.

I live in the moment when I'm with Zane, and until I met him, I didn't know how happy I could be with that type of lifestyle. I'm not so sure I want to go back to the way things were.

"You've got to be kidding me," Jake snaps. "All for this guy?"

"This guy?" I ask. "You mean my boyfriend, Zane?"

"Come on, Willa, you really think you two will end up together?"

"Yeah, I do."

I slam the coffee down and spin on my heel.

"Wait, okay, that was uncalled for." Jake follows me. "I'm sorry. I just, he came out of nowhere."

I stop at the sincerity in his voice.

"I'm sorry," he repeats. "I just sort of thought you and I … well, that we would end up together one day."

What? Is he serious?

My face must mimic my thoughts.

"I know. I know. This isn't right for me to say while you're dating someone."

"No, it's not."

"I just feel like I should tell you anyway. Maybe it will … I don't know."

"Change my mind?"

"Maybe."

"It won't."

"Okay, fine, but that doesn't change the fact that you and I running the Cali clinic are the perfect duo, Willa. Come on. Don't pass on it just yet."

I let out a sigh and turn to face him.

"You've worked so hard for this, so don't give it up yet."

I can't find the words because he's not wrong. I did work for this. I worked hard. But leaving Zane doesn't feel right either.

"I'm sorry, and if your choice really is not to go, then okay. I accept it. But could I still run a few ideas by you for the new clinic? Your input would be fantastic, and honestly, no matter who they choose to replace you, well, they won't be even half as amazing."

"That's kind of you to say."

"So, what do you say? Dinner this weekend? You can tell me how horrible my ideas are, then tell me how to improve them."

I smile at this because I do actually have some stellar ideas.

"Just dinner?"

He nods.

"To talk about work?"

He nods again.

"I think I can handle that."

"Great." He winks before heading down the hall. "I'll text you the details."

Just because I'm not going doesn't mean I can't help from here.

This is actually good. I'm still a part of the clinic.

That's good enough, right?

CHAPTER TWENTY-NINE
ZANE

I love watching Willa in her element. Right now, at the end of summer Best You's annual open-door event, she's shining brighter than ever. She could do this on her own. She's probably the most proficient at her job, and I'm not just saying that because she's my girl. I'm saying it because it's true.

I grab a mocktail; I think it's supposed to represent a mimosa. Non-alcoholic wine or something is in it. Honestly, after the last event I went to with this group, I'm sort of wishing this were real alcohol, but I get it. It's a free health and wellness tips day. The clinic answers questions, shows different types of stretches, and even provides sample meal plans to anyone who comes by. There are snacks and drinks and it's an all-day thing. I've heard of this before, but till I met Willa, I had no desire to stop by.

I take a sip just as Jake walks up next to me.

Because of course he would. This man hates me. I chuckle; if only he knew how Willa and I even came to be.

He leans one arm on the reception desk and crosses one ankle over the other as he sighs.

"She'd have been perfect for the job in Cali, man. It's too bad she couldn't take it."

Ah, he's cutting right to the chase. It's like he can sense that her picking me is a weakness of mine. And yet, I keep chanting *she made her choice. You didn't make it for her. She made it on her own. Respect it.*

"Yep," is all I say. Because he's right but moving isn't what she wants anymore.

"I'm sure things will work out for her, but to turn it down because she doesn't want to live in the sun and heat all year round is crazy. That sure as hell wouldn't be stopping me. I like the mountains, too, but not enough to stay here for them. I can visit."

Don't get worked up. Don't do it.

"She said she wasn't going because she didn't want to live in the sun all year round?" I ask.

He nods. "Yeah. She said Cali is too hot, and that she likes the mountains and the small-town feel of Wind Valley. Honestly, there has to be something else, but she never said."

I know he's trying to get under my skin, and as much as I also know I shouldn't let it happen, it does. Now, I didn't expect her to come right out and say that she wasn't leaving because of me, but she didn't even say she was staying to pursue her career in a new direction. Is she still planning on doing that? Or is she planning to give it all up to stay here, stagnant with Best You?

"You know," Jake goes on before I say another word, "I feel like I should apologize. I thought you and Willa were more of a fling." He shakes his head. "I would have never asked her out had I known the two of you were this serious about each other. I—oh, there's my sister. I'll see you around, Zane."

My next drink is dry, and I have to force it down as it sticks in my throat.

I didn't know you two were this serious.

Are we?

Of course we are, and if we are, shouldn't I offer to move with her? I write novels for a living. I can do that anywhere.

If I suggest moving with her, then this … us … it's real. Like *real* real.

* * *

As soon as we get to her apartment, I stop in the doorway.

"Everything okay?" she asks slowly.

I nod, but then quickly shake my head. "You have to take the job, Willa."

She sighs, dropping her purse on the table by her door and crossing her arms. "I'm not going over this again. I'm not taking it. I want to be here with you."

"I can't let you pass up on your dream job for a man. It's not right."

"I'm not passing it up for you. I'm passing it up for me and what I want. I promise. Besides, what did you want me to say? I'm not taking it because I met this guy, and I don't …"

She stops talking and shakes her head.

"So I am the reason?"

"Not the only one."

She's saying the words, but I can't process them the way she wants. In the end, if she hadn't met me, she'd be going.

I lived the last two years upset that a woman didn't pick me, and now one is, and I can't let her do it. It doesn't feel right.

"You have to go."

She bits her bottom lip and sighs. "I'm not going, Zane. When will you accept that?"

"When I know you aren't doing it for me."

"I'm not." Her hands swing into the air in defeat. "I'm tired of this conversation, Zane."

"Then look me in the eye and tell me you don't want that job."

"I do want that job, but—"

Something stabs at my chest before she finishes, a thought that never occurred till right this moment.

"Then why wouldn't you ask me to go with you?"

"I …"

I give her a minute, maybe two to find her words. I know it isn't long, but it feels like an eternity.

"If I had suggested it, you would have freaked out, and I didn't want to do that."

I can feel my eyes bug out as I look at her. "You didn't want to freak me out."

"Moving for someone else is a big commitment, and it took me this long to convince you to date me. I wasn't about to ruin all the progress I made by—"

"Whoa, whoa, whoa, back up. Are you dating me because you actually want to be with me or because I was some experiment you wanted to see if you could change?"

Like before, she hesitates.

"Wow." I jerk my keys off her counter and head for the door.

"Zane, stop. You're misreading all of this. I wasn't trying to do anything but show you that you can be loved and be in love. Do you really think I'd give up a job for a guy who I saw only as an experiment?"

"So I was?"

"Oh my god, you're not listening to me, Zane."

"You know, I don't think people who want to be together are supposed to fight like this or mistrust each other."

She shrugs. "Even the happiest couple fights from time to time."

"Take the job or don't. I don't care anymore."

Her gaze narrows and then she laughs. "I see what you're doing. It's not going to work on me, Zane Rosey. You can try to make me mad and push me away, but it won't work."

Is that what I'm doing?

I swallow as she settles on her couch, ready to pick out a movie. Her hand is shaking as she lifts the remote and then she stands again.

Tears are rolling down her cheeks.

I can see her fighting it. I can see that she wants to open up and say more to me, but she doesn't want to say the wrong thing.

Neither do I. Most importantly, I don't want to do the wrong thing.

I love her, but she deserves better and more than what I can offer her: a heart that refuses to accept that everything will be okay.

"I told you I didn't want commitment," I say slowly and this, this is what grabs her attention. "If I'm being honest, this was great. It was. Super fun, but it's been a distraction I can't afford anymore, and it's better for me if we end things."

"You're just making that up, so I'll argue with you and then go to Cali in the end."

I let out a deep breath. "I wanted you to pick Cali because if you did, then I didn't have to end this. You'd end it, and I wouldn't look like the bad guy."

She slowly rises from the couch.

I avoid looking at her and put my hand on the doorknob.

"What are you doing?" she asks. She takes her steps as if she's approaching a stray kitten who could bolt at any moment.

"Look, Willa, I told you. I didn't want to have to do this, but you gave me no choice."

"Um, no. What the hell, Zane?"

I clearly underestimated her stubbornness.

"What about all your 'I can't live without you' speeches and kissing me with your "well this is an option" kiss and all that other stuff?"

I shrug. "I got caught up in the moment. That's all. I'll miss you, yeah, sure, but this will never last."

She jerks back like I slapped her.

"Wow."

I need to just walk out the door. Don't look back.

"Look at me and tell me that this has all just been a fling to you. That you don't want to be with me."

I do it before I can stop myself.

"I don't want to be with you."

"Get out. Get out right now."

I'm a so taken back by her tone that I don't move.

"Leave!" she screams, and this puts my ass in gear.

I walk out the door, and I don't look back.

CHAPTER THIRTY
WILLA

It doesn't take a rocket scientist to know that I have a broken heart. It's split right in two, and there isn't a surgeon on earth who can put it back together.

Only Zane.

No, screw that. Me. I'm the one who can put it back together.

Yet Zane could help.

If he could just pull his head out of his ass and talk to me.

When he walked out two nights ago, I cried for a solid hour. Then I was numb. Then I started texting him. Not like a crazy stalker, but I don't believe him. Sort of. The part about just being a fling. He freaked out, and that's how he chose to deal with it. He just needs …

Wait, what am I doing? What Zane needs? What *Zane* needs? What about what I need?

I need someone who believed in me, in us, and I didn't get that from him.

Zane was never the reason I didn't take the job. He was

part of the reason, sure, but not the entire reason. Zane helped me see what I really wanted and where I really wanted to be. That's all. I would have stayed in Wind Valley whether or not he and I worked out. Which, it seems, we didn't.

"Do you need more of a break?" Greer says, poking her head into the break room.

"Before what?" I ask, checking my watch. My next appointment shouldn't be here for another fifteen minutes.

"Well," she looks over her schedule and steps in, closing the door behind her. "Jake has been out here rehearsing what he's going to say to you."

"For what?"

Her face cringes. "I may have let it slip that you and Zane broke up, and now he's determined to get you to come to Cali."

"Why does everyone think I need to be in Cali? Doesn't anyone think I can make my own choices?"

"I know you can. I also know that it's not an easy choice to make."

I blow out a breath.

"Anyway, I just wanted you to be prepared when—"

"Willa, there you are," Jake says in a breath, as if he'd been searching for me for days.

Greer covers her grin with her hand and leaves.

"What's up, Jake?" I keep eating the soup in front of me. I slurp it and then let out a giggle.

Two months ago, I wouldn't have been caught dead slurping soup in front of Jake, let alone casually asking him what's up and not looking forward to whatever he has to say.

Fuck love. When it doesn't work out, it ruins everything.

"I … I'm going to be blunt," he says and pulls out the

chair across from me. "I heard you and Zane broke it off, and I was hoping that means you would change your mind about Cali and possibly about me."

"About you? Did I think of you poorly?"

Another slurp.

"No. But seeing you with Zane sparked something inside of me that I didn't know was there, and I'd really like to explore a relationship with you as more than friends."

The soup in my mouth almost sprays all over him.

"You're serious?" I say as I wipe my mouth off. "We just broke up, Jake."

"Yeah, well, I don't like to see you hurting."

All right, I'll give him that.

"If not now, later. I just want you to know where I stand. But I also don't want this to affect your choice in taking this job. No one else can do what you do, Willa. I want this place to be successful, and I can't do that without you. Please reconsider."

It's nice to hear when you're appreciated, and with recent events, this was a great time for someone to share them with me.

"I don't know, Jake. There have been a lot of changes in the last couple of months that I'm still trying to process."

"I get it, I do." He stands up. "Just … I know this is something you want. You've worked hard for it, and with everything that's going on, maybe this choice is the easiest one for you to make. This one could just be for you."

If I could make one choice for myself, it wouldn't be moving for a job. It would be to fall into Zane's arms and never leave, but that's no longer an option. You know what is an option? Refusing to let anyone control my choices. I know what I want, dammit, and I'm sick of people standing in my way.

So I guess it does make my decision easy.

I nod. "You're right. This is the easiest choice I can make. I'm going to put in my two weeks' notice."

"What? Willa, are you serious?" He rushes toward me, eyes wide and lips turned down. "That's not what—"

"Thank you for helping me figure it out," I say and wrap him in a hug.

"Your next appointment is here," Greer says, holding the door open.

I'm still smiling and holding on to Jake when my eyes meet the man standing at the reception desk.

He holds no expression, he just stares.

Now, I don't know Simon very well outside of our relationship here at Best You, but as one of Zane's closest friends, I can see in his eyes that he knows everything.

I don't jump from Jake's arms or even act as if I'm sad he caught me. I'm not doing anything wrong.

If anything, I'm doing exactly what Zane told me to do.

If anyone has a problem, it should be him and not me.

I hold my head up as I leave the break room and wave for Simon to follow me to my office. We conduct our appointment in a professional manner, and I'm proud of myself for holding it together.

Yet once he leaves, I can't control the tears. Even people who take back control can have a shattered heart.

CHAPTER THIRTY-ONE
ZANE

Zane

The last two weeks have been the worst two weeks of my entire life.

And I've had broken bones, I've had books tank, I've been cheated on, and I've had repeated rejections from publishers, and yet, losing Willa hurts more than all of that combined.

My fingers fly over the keyboard.

I've taken advantage of my wounded heart and set a new record on how fast I can write a book. Two weeks for eighty thousand words in a new book.

"Hello?" a voice calls out from somewhere in my house. It's Simon. I'm not surprised. Beck has been occupied by a book he can't write and has been holed up in his new basement office or at the gym. He probably has no idea Willa and I broke up. Which is fine. He's my best friend, but he has a life too. Not to mention I haven't reached out to any of the guys since I walked out of her apartment.

"Zane, you here?"

"In the back room," I say and save my work.

He steps into my bedroom and then backs up.

"What the fuck is that smell?"

"Don't be so dramatic."

"Dude, I'm not, and I'm a little shocked as hell right now. We write this scene, you know, the broken-hearted hero who, for some reason always turns smelly when he's sad, but I never thought I'd actually see it."

"Glad I could bring that moment to life for you."

He chuckles. "Seriously though, you should take a shower."

"I need to finish this book."

"The best friend's ex one that you still need a title for?"

"Nope, I finished that one the night Willa and I broke up. This is a new one. I'm going to squeeze one more release into my schedule for this year."

"Fuck," he says, the *k* rolling longer than normal. "This is bad."

You're fucking right it is.

"Have you tried to talk to her?" he says as he disappears into the hall, coming back a moment later with my Lysol. He sprays it as he walks into the room.

"It's not that bad."

"Smell yourself."

To please him, I grab my shirt and sniff.

Holy fucking sweaty balls.

I meet his gaze and then move my computer off my lap. "Give me five minutes."

"I'll give you ten."

Freshly showered, I retreat into my kitchen where Simon has sandwiches and beers ready on the table.

"You are a lifesaver," I say and take a seat across from the sandwich not in front of him.

"Yeah, well, we leave for Billings in the morning, so I need you to be in a state that's easy to be around. This was a purely selfish visit."

I shrug. "Either way, thank you."

"Also, how are things with you and Willa?"

Mid-bite, I drop my sandwich and grab my beer.

"There is no me and Willa."

"Still?"

"What do you mean, *still*? Like that was going to change?"

"Yes, exactly like that."

"She deserves better than me!" I snap.

Simon groans and sets his sandwich down. "You're really going with that sad, sorry excuse? Damn, that's a tale as old as time. Did she say she wanted better than you?"

Like a child, I roll my eyes. "She didn't have to. I could feel it. I could feel myself getting into my head. Once I got far enough, she'd see me for who I was and walk away. I had to do it first."

From the corner of my eye, I can see him shaking his head.

"You're going to let her go? Just like that?"

I let out a long sigh and nod. I can't keep going in circles over this. Willa and I are over. That's it.

"Did you get that, ugh, um, that," I wave my hand in front of my face as I fail to find my words, "shit, I can't even remember where you were in your latest WIP. Did you finish it?"

"Look, I know you don't want to talk about it, but I think you need to. If not with me, then someone else. Maybe Beck?"

I shake my head. "Beck wouldn't be talking to me this calmly. He's all about fighting for the girl, and I tell you what, when he does meet her, she won't stand a chance. Sadly, his passion for commitment won't help me."

"Why not?"

"It was never going to last."

"You don't know that."

"But I do. When we started this whole thing, it was all for show, and then it was something to do to pass the time till she got this job. It wasn't supposed to be serious. No matter how blurred the lines got."

"This is going to be a stupid question, but did you both actually say it wasn't serious in the end?"

My brows dip as I try to make sense of what he means. I can't figure it out, and thankfully, he doesn't make me wait long.

"Okay, you both said 'let's have fun,' and at some point, you both knew it was more, right? The lines blurred, like you said, and neither of you called it quits when it got there. That's like the universal sign for 'let's be together no matter what.'"

I shake my head. "Not for us."

"Why are you fighting this?"

"Because she deserves better!" I yell. "They all do in the end. I won't be enough. It's better this way."

Simon nods slowly and stands.

"Just because one woman didn't think you were enough for her doesn't mean they all will."

I ignore him and keep eating.

"It takes two people to create a relationship filled with love, but it takes only one of those people to break it. If I were you, I'd think good and hard whether she's the person you want to be with. Willa does deserve better, but not from someone else. She deserves it with you, because unless she outright told you to fuck off, you're the person she wants. End of story."

He grabs his unopened bag of chips off the counter and walks out my front door.

If that line came from anyone but Simon, I'd think they were quoting one of their books. Simon isn't. He's the only one in the group who has ever had love worth fighting for and lost it.

He knows a pain worse than I'll ever imagine.

So I let his words sink in.

I want to be the good guy. The right guy. The perfect guy for Willa.

It's just not that easy for me.

CHAPTER THIRTY-TWO
WILLA

I'm in a daze.

I have friends and family in various rooms of my apartment, helping me pack.

I sigh, looking out the front window.

I've done a lot of thinking in the past couple of weeks. Most of it over the last conversation Zane and I had.

Did I try to change him? Yeah, sure. I didn't do it for myself, though. I wanted him to change for him. So he could see his self-worth. Turns out, no matter how much you care for someone, you can't change someone who doesn't want it.

Nope.

I can, however, change the way I control my choices.

The tape gun in Greer's hand screeches over the box she's closing. She spots me watching her and smiles.

It's a sad smile.

I move my attention to Calla, who is shoving books in a box and glaring at me.

"This. Is. Dumb," she says. "I move here in like two

weeks and you're leaving. Who am I supposed to be friends with?"

"Um, me?" Greer offers with a laugh.

Calla laughs too. "You know what I mean."

They both start chatting about what they're going to do next weekend. "You both know I'm only moving across town, right?"

"Yeah, but this place was so conveniently near my brother's," Calla says.

"And to my apartment." Greer shrugs.

I shake my head and smile. It's not the forced smile that most of them have been lately.

My phone rings across the room, so I move toward it, answering when my brother and nephew's picture appears.

"Hey, did you get it?' I ask. Austin ran out for tape, but he's been gone for almost an hour.

"Sorry, I had to make a stop, and now I need to get the kids from the babysitter. I won't be back for a bit. The sitter wants to talk about a new schedule. Can you go get the tape?"

"Yeah, of course. See you later."

"Bye, Willa."

I hang up.

"I'll be back," I tell the girls, grabbing my purse.

"Where are you going?" Calla asks, rushing to the entrance with Greer hot on her heels.

"To get more tape," I answer.

"Perfect! Get wine too."

"Be back soon," I say with a laugh and dash out the door.

It doesn't take me nearly as long as I'd like to make it in and out of the store, so I choose to walk down Main Street.

At the beginning of the summer, all I could focus on was

the promotion that was right at my fingertips. Now, I'm moving out of my apartment because I can't afford it without a full-time job, and I'm slowly starting my own business online. Someday, I'll have a shop of my own, but for now, this is the stage I'm in and no one has a say but me.

It's perfect.

Career-wise, I'm all set.

Now Zane-wise … I choke up just thinking of him and stop to take a breath. He's everything I didn't know I needed. I should go talk to him. Smooth things over before I carry out too many fake conversations about how things could have gone in my head, but I can't do it. I'm not saying he was right. But he wasn't wrong either. We did give this thing between us a timeline, and we never really established what we were. I sort of thought it was implied, but knowing him, he needed the actual words and I—

My train of thought cuts off when I look up at the "available for rent" sign in the window in front of me.

It's a studio office just down the street from The Black Alcove bar. I glance around. Has this always been vacant?

I lean forward, cupping my hands around my eyes as I peek inside the space.

"Looking to rent?"

I jump back and find a man in a T-shirt and jeans. I eye him up and down. He looks friendly enough, and then he smiles, reaching into his back pocket and handing me a business card.

Oh, he must own the building.

"Looking to rent?" he asks again.

"Possibly."

"Want to take a look?" He holds up some keys.

My gaze flickers between the keys and the space, and I smile.

"Oh, wow. If you have time, I'd love to look at it."

"Great. I have plenty of time."

He unlocks the door, and we step inside.

"What kind of store are you opening?"

"Not a store exactly. More a place to do some one-on-one nutrition consulting and maybe have a little studio in the back for fitness workouts."

He snaps his fingers. "Something more personal than all those big guys and clinics. I think that's brilliant."

I smile and step farther into the empty space.

"So do I."

His phone rings, so he excuses himself to step outside and tells me to take my time.

And I do. I start at the back where there is a small space with a sink and half counter. I could easily add to this and make it a mini kitchen. Oh, I could offer a meal prep service too.

Next, I move toward the middle where I could easily have a couple of machines like a treadmill or a rower set up. Get a camera for recording, and I could have a desk toward the front for natural light. I'd be right in the heart of downtown Wind Valley doing exactly what I want.

My heart races, and my eyes water.

"So, what do you think?" He comes back in and tucks his phone away.

"How soon can we do the paperwork?" I ask, and he laughs.

We discuss the paperwork and banking and all that goes

into renting a space—I could have this in my name by the end of next week.

I do my best not to speed on the way back to my place. I run through the door and toss the tape on the couch.

"I just signed a lease on a storefront downtown!"

Greer and Calla freeze and then both erupt into cheers.

"You're getting everything you wanted," Greer says, enveloping me in a hug. Calla is right behind her.

"Almost everything," I say and grin. "There is just one thing left."

With the pieces of owning my own business falling into place, it's true—there is only one thing left that I want.

The guy.

More specifically, Zane Rosey.

And if I learned anything about that man over the last couple of months, it's that he's never had anyone fight to keep him.

Till now.

CHAPTER THIRTY-THREE
ZANE

When my agent offered to toss in a last-minute signing one state over in Billings, I didn't hesitate to take it. I needed out of Wind Valley. Heck, I needed to get out of the state. Simon and his little speech have left my mind reeling. All I can think about is that even though I think she deserves better than me, there isn't a single guy out there who knows her worth more than me.

Fuck, it's a hamster wheel inside my head, so yeah, I had to get out of town.

"Okay, run this by me again. We are at this signing together because you don't know what you want?"

I nod, refusing to look at Hero and Beck, who are both glaring at me. "I know what I want. It's what I—"

"Need I remind you of how I lost the girl?" Hero asks. "Because I thought dreams were more important."

"No," I stand to correct him, "you lost the girl because she deserved better. This is the same thing. Better for Willa is not picking me over herself. End of story."

"I get it," Beck chimes in. "But I don't. That's her choice. You can't take that from her."

"I didn't. I merely suggested she not pick me, and she didn't argue."

"Yeah, she did," Beck laughs. "You just told us about it."

"It doesn't matter."

"It does. Why couldn't you just go with her from the start again? That could have really helped you two sidestep this whole fight."

"Say I moved with her and down the road I'm not what she wants—then what? I just move back? Moving is a big step. It's a full-on commitment that has no guarantee it won't end in disaster."

"Now we are getting somewhere." Beck's face lights up as he claps and moves to sit in front of me. "You're scared. It's simple. You. Are. Scared. And you broke it off with her before she could break it off with you. Typical."

"You're wrong. I'm not scared."

But the last part of his statement … that isn't too far off. After all, I said those exact words to Simon.

"Okay, so if you two weren't fighting, what would you be doing right now?"

Truth be told, I'd probably be freaking out a little about how lucky I was. To find the perfect woman for me and have everything work out the way I want … yeah, right.

"I'd be right here, signing books with you and the guys. Doing what I'm meant to be doing. This is the end of this discussion."

Beck groans. "The end, ha. You want this conversation to be over? Fine, you got it. You know what else is over? You and Willa, because you can't pull your head out of your ass and see what you have right in front of you. A woman who loves you. Damn. You are so freaking stubborn. Seriously, I barely know Willa, and just from this conversation and what Nora mentioned about Willa signing that lease downtown to start her own—"

"What did you just say?"

He freezes and keeps his focus anywhere but me.

"Nothing."

"No, what did you just say? Willa signed a lease in Wind Valley?"

"Umm."

"Beck, tell me what's going on. What do you know?"

"I'm not supposed to say anything."

"What do you mean, you're not supposed to say anything?"

His hands go up. "Exactly what it means."

"Just tell me already."

"Just tell him." Simon leans over, adding in his opinion. "The sooner he knows, the sooner we can move on."

"What's this *we*?" Beck asks. "Last I checked, it was only him and Wi—"

"Stop stalling."

"Fine. Fine. She quit her job and started her own thing. No matter what you two fought about, she isn't going anywhere."

Everything around me stops, including the pen in my hand. "She's still in Wind Valley?"

Beck nods. I look past him at Simon, who also nods. "She made her choice. She isn't going anywhere. Which is exactly what she said, isn't it?"

Fuck. I'm an idiot. A royal idiot.

"Crazy, isn't it?" he goes on before I can respond. "When

a person does exactly what they said. Hmm, makes you wonder what else she told you that was true."

"Stop. I get it."

"Do you?"

"Yes."

"Okay then. Now, the question is, what are you going to do about it?"

He's right. What am I going to do?

I spent so much time thinking that Willa wouldn't believe in me enough to stick around when things got hard, I didn't believe in her.

Whatever I do, it has to be right.

"Damn it!"

The woman in front of me shifts on her feet, and Beck clears his throat. "Just a tip, but the faster you sign and mingle with your readers, the sooner you are to driving home. Just saying."

I grin widely at the fan in front of me.

"Who do you want this made out to?" I ask.

Needless to say, my attitude improves for the rest of the afternoon, and after just two more hours, I'm on the road.

* * *

Not seeing her car should have been my first sign. It should have been the one to not even get out of my car. Not to walk up the pathway to her door. Not to peek into the window to see that everything is gone. Everything.

A completely vacant apartment stares back at me.

I'm not sure how long I stand there before I get in my car and drive home, not remembering the actual drive itself. It's scary how I can get from point A to point B without remembering it.

That's how gone for Willa I am.

Hell, I'm not a crier, but I could do it right now—in fact, I'm on the verge when I pull into my driveway.

I park my car and hop out, slamming the door harder than necessary.

What am I doing? I shouldn't be going home defeated. I should get back in my vehicle and go find her. I need to keep trying to reach her. Going home isn't going to do me any good.

I grab my driver's door handle and pause.

Okay, think clearly, Zane. Running around town like a madman till I find her won't work on Willa. I need a plan. A solid one. I need to think of the words I'm going to say to her. Write them down.

A love letter! Yes, that's what I need.

I turn, jogging to the door and jerking it open. The part of me that doesn't waste any time presses send to call her once more. She won't answer. She hasn't all day, but who can blame her? I messed up. I hurt her.

"Hey, it's Willa. Leave a message and I'll call you back."

I never left a voice mail before, but I will this time. I need all the help I can get.

Beep.

"Willa, it's Zane. Hell, you know that. Look, there isn't an easy way to say this, but I messed up. I said the wrong things, and I chose the wrong actions. I should have never walked out on you. I should have stayed, and I sure as hell should have listened when you told me what you wanted. I ... I let my fear of being left behind get the best of me, just like you called me out for, and I let that same fear take the best thing that's ever happened to me away from me. I … shit, I don't want to have this conversation on the phone, in a voice mail. Call me back, baby, please. I'm in love with you."

A gasp fills the air behind me. I spin on my heel.

Willa is standing only a couple steps away at the entrance to my kitchen.

Her hand covers her mouth as she stares at me. It takes me only a moment to process what just happened.

She heard everything. I don't move, and I don't speak. I wait for her to make the next move. She's here, so that means something. I need to give her a moment to share it with me before I jump to conclusions. Clearly, doing that has never worked for me before.

I thought about what Beck said. The whole 'you broke it off before she could' thing. He was right. I let my panic of not being someone's first choice ruin all the opportunities Willa and I could have.

Well, my lucky ass is getting one more, and I'm not letting it pass, because the best thing that has ever walked into my life is right in front of me. She's here. In my living room.

"I'm sorry I had to sneak in. Well, actually, Calla took your spare key from her brother's house, but what did you expect?" She shrugs. "I know how to get what I want … sort of." She sets the plate of cookies in her hand down on the kitchen table. "I know what you said that night in my apartment, but I'm not going anywhere." She fidgets, looking at the floor before she glances up with a smile. "I had this whole 'what we have is once in a lifetime. Deep down, I know you know it, too' speech planned out, but I sort of feel like it's a moot point, you know. Now that I just heard the voice mail you left me."

I take one step, still not talking.

"Do you really love me?" she asks in a rush and holds up her hands. "Wait, that was silly, don't—"

"I'm in love with you, Willa," I blurt out before she can say another word. I'm pretty sure I knew where she was going with the rest of her sentence, but I really wanted to say it again. "I love you with all my heart, and I'm not going to stop. What I said the other night was a lie. I was scared you wouldn't pick me or that I wouldn't be what you needed. Turns out, the idea of losing you scares me more than anything else."

Her bottom lips shakes, and she reaches up slowly, touching it as if she wants to stop it from moving.

"You love me?" she asks, this time with disbelief in her tone. I get the feeling she came here thinking she'd have to put up more of a fight for us.

"More than anyone in this world."

"You really do?" she asks in a flirty tone while stepping closer to me, and I let out a deep chuckle.

"Yes."

"Good," she says, her face turning calm, and she nods. "Because I love you, too, and this will only work if we are on the same page."

"Oh," I say, moving toward her once again, reaching out to grab the apron she's wearing and tug her toward me. "We are on the same page."

I pull her in for a kiss, and I swear the color comes back into my world with just one touch.

"Good. Good. Because, um, I sort of moved in while you were gone the last couple of days."

"What?"

"I can pack it all up, but I was really banking on knowing you more than you know yourself. I was ready to fight for you, for us. I was ready to do everything I could to prove that this is right. You and me."

"Hold on, hold on." I shake my head and step back to look at her. Then I swing my gaze over the kitchen at the things she's added. "You're telling me that not only did I get the girl I'm in love with back, but she's here to stay?"

She shrugs shyly and nods. "Yes."

I don't know if she planned to say more, but if she did, I don't give her the chance. I swoop in, slide my hand around her hips, then lift her up on the counter. My hands go to her knees as I spread her legs apart and stand between them.

"Wait, what about your job?" I ask.

She beams a smile. "You are now looking at the proud lease owner of a spot in downtown Wind Valley for my own nutrition and fitness business."

"Are you kidding me, Willa? That's incredible."

I smash my lips to hers and pull back to ask more, but the heated gaze she gives me is all I need. Right now we need the same thing and talking about work isn't it.

I capture her mouth with mine, diving my tongue between her lips to tangle with hers, and on a moan, her hips roll over my growing erection.

This counter isn't ideal, but hell, we are about to have sex all over this house, so this is only the beginning.

Her fingers reach between us and fumble with the zipper of my jeans.

"I missed you so much," she says on a breath, and the words course through my body like a drug.

"I love you so much," I say, running my lips over her neck and chest before grabbing the hem of her shirt and lifting it over her head. She repeats the same for me and drops my jeans and briefs to my knees. I left her butt off the marble and peel off her shorts.

God, I'll never get over her small lips or how soft her skin is. I grow harder just knowing that from this moment on, she will be right in my reach.

I pull back just enough to position myself right at her entrance. She bites her lip and digs her heels into my ass as she tugs her body closer to mine, my shaft disappearing inch by inch.

This isn't just sex with Willa. It's a connection. It's trust. It's me giving her my everything with just a simple act. Although getting to this point was anything but simple.

Still, in the end, no matter what we went through, we made it.

I pump my hips slowly at first, speeding up only when she meets me thrust for thrust. She grabs hold of my shoulders to hold on.

"Oh, hell, Zane. I'm going to … shit … shit!"

"Willa," I groan out as the slapping of our bodies grows quicker and faster, her release hitting her hard as she bites my shoulder and I grab her ass to hold her still while my body reaches its own climax.

Slowly, we ride out wave after wave of pleasure before she collapses into my chest.

She doesn't get to relax long before a flame erupts on the stove.

"Oh shit!" she squeals and pushes me away, dashing naked from the hips down to contain the fire. I'm right behind her, taking the on-fire pan and tossing it into the sink.

She looks at me with wide eyes. "Dinner out?"

I chuckle and hand her her shorts.

She shoots a cheeky grin my way.

"What?" I ask, buttoning my own pants.

"Nothing."

"Tell me." I don't care how cheesy I am. I wrap my arms around her and kiss her forehead. "Tell me."

"I found this today," she says, holding up a piece of paper. It's the goals worksheet from her retreat.

"Ah," I say, knowing exactly what I wrote on it.

"Weakness," she reads, "Willa Boston."

I chuckle.

"Strength," she reads and starts to cry, "Willa Boston."

The first tear slips over her cheek, and I pull her to me and swipe it away.

"This feels good," she says.

"What? Us?"

"Yes. And coming here and taking the chance that you wouldn't turn me away just shows that I was right about you all this time."

I chuckle and squeeze her hard.

I'm sure as hell glad she was too.

EPILOGUE
BECK

The music is loud, the drinks are cold, and the food is overflowing.

This is the perfect way to celebrate owning my first house.

"Who ate the last piece of cake?" Tobias, one of my best friends, almost shouts over the long wooden table on my patio. It seats eight, but there are enough chairs pulled up right now to seat at least twelve of us.

"Um," Natalie, a good friend, and Tobias's best friend, is the only one to answer.

I watch as Tobias's gaze flashes to her and she shoves the last piece of white cake into her mouth.

His eyes go wide. "You did not just do that."

Mouth full, Natalie says, "Do what?"

Tobias's chair scratches back as he stands and Natalie does the same before she darts off into the yard, Tobias hot on her heels.

Typically, I or one of the guys from my tight group friends

would comment on this interaction. We'd either make smart-ass comments on how those two should be dating already or taking bets on which one of them is going to figure it out first, but not tonight. Tonight, Natalie's boyfriend, Griffin, is with us and is watching, calmly might I add, as another man chases his girl around the backyard.

It's weird if you ask me, but no one asked me, so I'll probably just turn up the music and change the subject.

Deep down, though, I want to tell him to at least pretend to be bothered or to talk to Natalie and tell her not to flirt with other guys in front of him. If he loves her, he needs to talk to her. I'd be questioning everything if I were in his shoes. Not to mention, he should be fighting for what he has with Natalie. He has someone to depend on. People spend their entire lives searching for someone, and he has it.

I'm not jealous. I *love* love, and I think more people should fight for what they want when they have it. Fight to keep and fight to fix any issues they have that keep them from being happy. Finding the right person isn't something people should take lightly. Ever.

"Numb" by Marshmello and Khalid rings through the back speakers I had installed this morning. My new house is two levels with a walkout basement that leads to the giant patio we are all sitting on, and since it sits on the river that runs through town, I have a half-acre backyard that extends all the way to the water. Living on the water is one of the many perks of my new place. In fact, the only downfall of the entire deal is that since it's still residential, the houses are too close together. The backyard is long, but if I stand up, I could see into my neighbor's yard and hold a conversation without even yelling. Well, I'd have to turn the music down, of course, but you get it.

"I'm so jealous that you live on the water," Nora, Hero's wife, says as she looks out over the water. "The summers will be amazing here."

"It's a good thing you're married to one of the owner's best friends, isn't it?"

Nora rolls her eyes. "It's a task no other woman could handle."

"Say something smart one more time and Natalie won't be the only woman out there running around the yard."

I glance at Natalie's boyfriend.

Still nothing.

When Nora doesn't say a word and her and Hero quickly fall into a whispered conversation between the two of them, I lean back, taking in all my friends. Some have found love in the last couple of years, some are still single, and then there is me. The one with the most complicated romantic life and no one to talk to about it. Seriously, where would I even begin? All that mumbo jumbo about fighting for love I wholeheartedly believe. Yet, when it comes to my own life, it's problematic.

Call me a romantic, that's fine. I don't write romance just for the hell of it or because it's the hottest market in book sales right now. I write it because I believe in it. I grew up with parents who still act like they just met. It's both sickening and amazing. I strive to find the kind of—

"For the love of god, can someone turn that horrid music off already?"

I click the music to mute and twist in my seat toward the

voice walking out my back door. I'd recognize it anywhere, and the goose bumps it gives me are the good tingly kind.

"Who invited you?" I snap and then look around the table.

"That would be me," Simon says, following his sister, Calla, out of the house. His son Grey is right behind him.

"You need better taste in music," Calla says and makes a gag face.

"Clearly, I need better taste in friends." I glare at Simon.

He laughs and takes a seat at the table.

"Here's a thought: with Calla moving to Wind Valley and you both living here and me being a middle factor, what if the two of you got along?"

Neither Calla nor I answer.

Be friends with Calla Stone?

That's never going to happen.

Complicated doesn't even begin to describe our relationship.

There was one time when we got along. It was brief, and it was pretty damn great. I take a swig of my beer and glance at Calla, who isn't looking my way.

Even after that drink, my throat goes dry thinking about that night with her.

Then I chuckle and shake the memory from my mind.

Calla and me … ha. That's a story for another day.

What happens when Beck's best friend's little sister moves in with him and they have a secret that could change everything?

Find out in the next Lust or Bust book, The Write Choice!

Want more from Zane and Willa?
Here's an exclusive bonus epilogue to make you swoon!

Reading in paperback? Just scan the QR below to join my
newsletter and get access to all my bonus scenes!

BONUS EPILOGUE
12 YEARS LATER

Zane

If there was ever a time I knew without question that I did something right, it was this moment right here.

"I said give me two, not one."

"You don't need two. You can only make one at a time."

"I don't care. I want two marshmallows."

"And I said—"

"Ben, give your sister two marshmallows," Willa says as soon as she steps out of the camper. Her hands are on her hips as she stares down our two children. Ben is nine now going on thinking he's CEO of the Rosey household, and Bridget is eight. Yes, even though we planned for two kids having them back-to-back like that was a shock.

Although, was it? To this day Willa and I still can't keep our hands to ourselves and if you didn't know us, you'd think we might be newlyweds. I mean, look at her, standing there with the late afternoon sun making her glow. She's wearing cut-off jean shorts with her mauve t-shirt tied at the waist and her hair is in a messy bun. It didn't stand a chance after I'd had my way with her this morning.

"She's going to make a mess and then we will both get in trouble and then you'll take the smores away and then—"

"Hey now, that's not true. You can't predict how something will turn out before it happens," I say. I almost follow it up with trust me, I would know, but I don't. Instead, I go with. "Listen to your mom and share with your sister, please."

As soon as Ben hands her the second marshmallow, Bridget smiles.

"Thank you."

Ben is about to start another argument, I can see it in the way he sat up higher and squared his shoulders. So, I stand and move toward the camper.

Yes, even though my kids are fighting, the fact we are here and they are happily enjoying the outdoors makes me happy. And even though they won't admit it, they love spending time with me and their mother. Creating a home and family that does that for them means I did something right.

It also means sometimes letting them argue and figure things out on their own.

I step into the camper to find Willa organizing the large space and getting everything ready for the week we are going to be out here.

We have a camper big enough to have two slide-outs, a kitchen island, bunk beds, a bathroom, a living room slash dining area, and a master bed.

I'm not sure if this still qualifies as camping to most people, but it does to me.

I move into the kitchen, stand behind Willa, and wrap my

arms around her. Then, I slowly start dragging her toward the master room.

"Zane," she slaps my hand. "We have things to do if we—"

That's all she gets out before I spin her and press my lips to hers.

"All I need is five minutes."

"And we have two kids outside who, if they walk in here, will be scarred for life."

My head falls back on a chuckle. "Those same two kids are unsupervised with a full bag of chocolate and marshmallows. They are going to be busy for at least twenty minutes."

"Mmm," she says with a knowing smile and then sits back on the bed.

"You better be quick."

I capture her mouth with mine once again and crawl over her as I unbuckle my pants.

"Mom!" Bridget yells. "How many is too many before dinner?"

I groan.

Just when I think I have my kids figured out, they remind me that I do not.

"I'll have your father get dinner ready now."

Willa lets out a breath as I zip my pants and sit next to her. "Did you put the blue cooler in the back of the truck?" She asks.

My brows rise. "I thought you did that. I put the red one in the back."

We look at each other and it doesn't take long to put the pieces together.

"We forgot the blue cooler," we say at the same time.

"Which cooler is that again?" I ask.

"The one with the meat in it."

"No," I shake my head. "I wouldn't forget that one. One camping trip without meat is enough for me in my lifetime."

"Well, now it's two."

"Shit."

Willa smiles and lets out a small laugh. "I mean … we could always sneak back to town real quick for some burgers."

I smile big.

My little sexy nutritionist has a weak spot for a greasy burger and I love it.

I love her.

I got so damn lucky.

"When did Nora say they would be here?" I ask.

She looks at her watch. "Maybe in a couple of hours."

I nod.

We're making a week of it with the entire crew and luckily, we are the first ones here.

"Alright, let's do it. I can text one of the guys to swing by our place for the cooler before they leave, too."

She stands and I smack her ass, earning a laugh as she moves back into the kitchen.

"Watch yourself, Mr. Rosey."

I wink. "The only thing I'm watching is you, Mrs. Rosey."

I grab her hand before she makes it too far and pull her back for one more kiss.

"Gross!" Both our kids say as they both fake gagging and press their fingers to their eyes from outside the camper door.

Willa and I laugh which only makes me kiss her again with more theatrics.

Ten minutes later, our entire family is loaded in the truck to go get some food. I grab my wife's hand from across the center console and kiss the back of it.

It's not quite the same as sneaking out like Willa and I did that first night we spent together.

It's better.

This time we aren't faking it.

This time … we're forever.

***

What happens when Beck's best friend's little sister moves in with him, and they have a secret that could change everything?

Find out in the next Wind Valley book, The Write Choice!

CHAPTER TWENTY-EIGHT
ZANE

Book signings in Vegas are always wild, but thankfully we finished the last one a couple of hours ago and are winding up the day writing poolside before we catch the red-eye flight back to Wind Valley.

I'm writing like a madman with more inspiration than I know what to do with, and Beck, well, he's huffing and puffing so hard I feel like his computer is going to end up in the water.

"Is something on your mind?" I ask without looking up.

"Everything is fine."

Yikes.

"Sounds fine."

"I just …"

"Hey, guys, do you want to get dinner with me, Grey, and Calla before the flight?" Simon asks, laying out a towel next to us, clearly with no plans of writing this afternoon. Grey does a cannonball into the water in front of us, and Beck twists and turns like he's trying to swat a bug or something away from him.

"Is she with you?"

Simon and I share a look, but I can't read too much into it before he slides his sunglasses on.

"She's getting a massage. She said she had a long night and needs to clear her head."

"Unbelievable," Beck snaps and I laugh. Beck doesn't like my reaction one bit.

"What? What's so funny?"

"Do you have a thing for Calla?"

"What? Do you like my sister? Dude, isn't there an unspoken pact on dating friends' sisters?"

"Is there?" Beck asks and then quickly shakes his head. "Doesn't matter. I don't like your sister."

He ducks his head and pinches that spot between his eyes. I'm about to ask more about his super weird behavior, but Simon changes the subject.

"Did you get that email from Doug about the retreat in Florida in a couple months?"

"Yep, I already told him I'm in," Beck says.

"A month-long writing retreat. Hell yeah, count me in," I say. "I'm emailing Doug right now to confirm."

"Don't you think you should talk to Willa about that?"

I look over the top of my screen at Beck. "Why would I need to talk to Willa?"

Beck rolls his eyes. "Come on, man. You know exactly why."

I shake my head. "Honestly, Willa is just as career hungry as I am. She'll understand."

"It might not be a bad idea," Simon adds.

"You better ask her," Beck snaps.

"Why?" I growl. There is a hint in his tone that I do not care for.

"Just hear me out. She gave up an entire job offer for you, and you can't even talk to her about a month-long work retreat. Sort of feels like one is giving more than the other."

I don't have anything to say. I hear him.

He goes back to writing as if his suggestion is something to be retained till I'm with Willa. But, nope, that's not how it happens.

No matter how she says it or how I say it, the fact remains that she isn't going to Cali so that we can have a chance together. And I'm letting her do that.

Fuck.

Am I ready for that? Am I ready to let someone make life choices based on what I want and don't want?

I swallow the dry lump in my throat.

Selfish people piss me off more than anything, and yet here I am, thinking nothing in my life has changed or will have to change, when everything she wants in life is.

I'm not so sure I can let her do that.

Any inspiration I have to write vanishes. I excuse myself and go to my room, pack my bag, and head to the airport much sooner than necessary.

All while thinking about how Willa is choosing me over her career. Up until this moment, I hadn't realized the pressure that puts on me.

There is no room for mistakes.

Am I ready for that?

Hell, what am I thinking? I'm freaking out because she isn't here for me to talk to. I need to get home, go to her, and all will be fine.

It has to.

No mistakes. Remember.

MORE BOOKS BY JAMI ROGERS

For the full list of titles by Jami Rogers, please scan the QR code below.

ACKNOWLEDGMENTS

Every book takes a team and I am forever thankful for mine!

Dana, Julie, Jenny, and Hang Le … I love working with you and I love the books we create.

Thank you for being on my side and continuously making my dreams come true.

To the readers who have read and loved my books, you have my heart and I wish I could thank each and every one of you one by one. Thank you for believing in me and loving my characters just as much as I do.

Cheers to the next book!

ABOUT THE AUTHOR

My name is Jami Rogers and I write new adult contemporary and adult contemporary romance novels. I *love* love and want to share my passion for happily ever afters with the world.

I was born in Wyoming and still live in the cowboy state with my husband, daughter, and two dogs. I like to read, write, run, watch movies/TV and spend time with my family. I'm horrible at returning phone calls and prefer to text, but still struggle to hit the little blue arrow to send a message once I'm finished typing my reply. My husband does 90% of the cooking in our house. Not because I'm busy – I'm just simply a bad cook.

Keep up with Jami by visiting her website www.
authorjamirogers.com
or
Sign up for Jami's newsletter so you don't miss out on book
news!

facebook.com/AuthorJamiRogers
instagram.com/jami_s_rogers
goodreads.com/jamirogers
bookbub.com/profile/jami-rogers
tiktok.com/@authorjamirogers

www.ingramcontent.com/pod-product-compliance
Lightning Source LLC
Chambersburg PA
CBHW061249310726

48971CB00007B/2288